EVERYONE PLAYS CHESS

VENI

BY FELIPE MORRIS

ISBN 13 : 9781506002545

ISBN 10: 1506002544

First Edition: January 2014

INTRODUCTION

We constantly ask, "Where are all the *good* black men and women?" Yet we are all searching for good inside of a 12" by 12" box. If we stop limiting ourselves to our specific social settings, we will begin to learn that good and bad lies in ALL people. Love, lust, and happiness have nothing to do with income status and educational background. Inside, you will find a tale of African American men and women, who through extreme circumstances, were forced to look outside of that box. Turn the page and take a peek into a world where there are no boundaries, and friendships, lovers, haters, and enemies emerge from all walks of life. Welcome to... Everyone Plays Chess.

ACKNOWLEDGEMENTS

First off, I would like to thank the universe for this blessing... I have always read that if you ask for something you shall receive it, so today I thank the universe for making me an author.

I'd like to thank all of the children in my life that inspire me to be better. There is nothing more motivating than having children look up to, and count on you.

Thank you Teff and Ferg for the design ideas and execution. When I told other graphic designers that I needed a cover for my book, they would play me as if I was joking, but you guys came through and made it happen.

I most definitely have to thank Tina aka my "Olivia Pope", for all that you do and all that you done, especially during the editing and execution process. There would be no "Everyone Plays Chess" without you.

I'd like to thank my Facebook friend list for allowing me to pick your brains from a distance, as well as the doctors, educators, and scholars that I correspond with via inbox.

To my closest cousin's whom I can call on for anything and to all of my loved ones thank you for your support.

Last but not least: Hassan, Muse, and Jeff, thank you for keeping me sane. Talking to you guys always reminded me that I'm not crazy lol.

To my family and loved ones, thank you for being there, and upon my mom's request, I would like to dedicate this book specifically to her and my children!

CHAPTER ONE

"SYLVIA AKA SYL"

"Sylvia stop, let her hair go!" Someone screamed from the crowd. Today would be the last time one of these big ugly bitches came down here fucking with her. Today, these hoes would learn! "Nah man! This bitch wanted a fight and now she got one!" Sylvia was tired of girls wanting to fight her over boys who she didn't even want! They were chasing her down because they had sucked some boys' dick who didn't even want them. They were all playing "Little Ms. Pleaser" to the guys, yet all of them came up the hill to stalk Sylvia. She didn't think about boys though... well... except for her protector, Bleed. All of this fighting over boys had to stop, and it would stop today.

Sylvia was using all of her weight to pull Big Renae down by her hair. Renae weighed at least 100 lbs. more than her but Sylvia had better technique. These hoes didn't know that she took karate three times a week, but they were about to find out! Sylvia started to feel her getting weaker and tired so she figured that it was time to make her move. She stood straight up while still holding her hair, stepped to the side, bent her back down, and flipped Renae's 250 lb. ass over her back and onto the ground! As soon as her big ass hit the ground, Sylvia started pounding her straight in the nose with hammer fist! When girls fought, they worried so much about their hair that they left their face open. Her fat ass was breathing as if she was having an asthma attack, well, maybe she was, but Sylvia didn't give a fuck, not today! She pulled back on Renae's hair, exposing her Adam's apple. When Renae reached for her arms to try and stop her from pulling her hair, she chopped her in the throat! She could have left it there but instead she started to knee her in the back. Her big ass fell flat on the ground holding her throat as if she was dying, but that didn't stop Sylvia! She kicked Renae in the face twice with her size 5 Timbs to make sure that she knocked her ass out cold. To finish her, she took her boot off and beat her in the face with it! Needless to say, this was the last time anyone, male or female, came for Sylvia. The brutal beating that she gave Renae even ran the boys away.

***

Sylvia Wright grew up on 13th street; a really rough part of Over the Rhine in downtown Cincinnati. She was beautiful, with light toned skin. Being 5'9" with a banging body at a mere age of sixteen, quite naturally, she always had beef with the girls in the hood over boys. Sylvia would boast that she stabbed or beat up at least 1 out of every 3 girls in the neighborhood. Being that she was a roughneck with obvious anger issues, it made perfect sense when she started hanging around Bleed, who was a local robbery boy. Despite her tough core, Syl was the pretty tomboy that all of the guys wanted, however, when they realized that she had no desire to be any of their girlfriends, they started calling her a lesbian. She wasn't mindful of her body, overall appearance, and the effects that it had on all the boys from her block, including some of the men. She found it hard to view herself as attractive. Things from her past made her feel ugly, dirty, and undesirable.

Meeting a young man like Bleed was a blessing for a little girl suffering from childhood trauma and abuse. When she was introduced to him by Ms. Geraldine, he seemed sincere in wanting to help her overcome her fears. Hearing that she had been sexually abused made him furious, now he wanted nothing more than to protect her, which is why he was hell-bent on teaching her how to also protect herself. He would always say that once she was old enough and absolved of her past hurt and anger, he was going to make her his wife. He stayed true to his promise. He never touched or even attempted to touch her in a sexual manner while she was still underage. Finally, at age eighteen, Sylvia had consensual sex with a twenty-four-year-old heartless thug named Bleed, and she loved his dirty drawers.

She would never forget that day; she was trying to play basketball with the boys, not even realizing that it was her birthday. Bleed pulled up in his truck with his friend Fred and motioned for her to come to him. "Happy Birthday baby girl! I want you to see what your hubby has in store for you." Bleed said. Fred hopped out and let Syl have the front seat. She was surprised! He never done that before. Bleed handed her a room key to a hotel that said *Sybaris Pool Suites* on the keychain.

"What is this key for?" She asked.

"Well me, you, Sharon and Fred are going there tonight. You and Sharon are going to ride up there right now. We have scheduled manicures, pedicures, and a massage for you both and after you finish up there, she is going to take you to the mall and show you how to start dressing like a young woman... MY woman. Hopefully you will let go of your tomboy ways," he explained. Sylvia laughed and he continued, "Me and Fred are going to ride up later after we handle some business here in the city."

Syl jumped for joy! She hadn't ever been on a road trip before... well... outside of riding the two hours that it took to get to Bleed's uncles cabin. Also, the thought of Sharon going with her was so exciting! Sharon was the neighborhood bad bitch. She was the girl that all of the other girls wanted to be, yet she was humble and easy to talk to. She was the person who Sylvia used to confide in after her mother's dope fiend boyfriends molested her. She helped her to get better and that was why she loved her some Big Booty Sharon.

***

Sylvia was molested at age twelve, and like most girls, she literally became afraid of men. She was even fearful of the boys her age because she felt that although they were little men they could do the same amount of harm. Prior to being molested, Sylvia was a happy and playful girl. You could always find her laughing or cracking jokes with the other girls on the block. Being molested changed her though, it made her feel dirty. It made her want to hide from everything and everyone. Her newfound reclusiveness caught the eye of Sharon, the bodacious chick from the block. Sylvia was sitting on a step away from all the other kids when Sharon walked over and sat next to her. "Lil Syl, I don't know how you were hurt or who hurt you, but I want you to know that you can come and talk to me. I can see that you have been going through something because everything about you has changed. You aren't taking the time to put your little outfits together like I taught you. You haven't even been taking care of your pretty hair." Sharon said while shaking her head. "Look at your nails... Your polish is all chipped up and that's just not you; I taught you better than that. Young ladies should never have chipped nail polish on their fingers or toes. Syl, you are beautiful and when you get older, men will kill for you. They will want to take care of you, and they will damn sure protect you. I see a lot of me in you, and you can get through this. I want you to meet my Aunt Geraldine. She took me in when I was in the same position as you. Don't allow the person that hurt you to make you feel dirty; they are the ones who are filthy. You don't have to talk right now, but when you are ready babe I will be all ears," she said with concern. Syl gave Sharon a nod and continued to stare at the ground.

It took her months to talk to Sharon. She even started to avoid her altogether because she felt that Sharon could see right through her. She just felt nasty and didn't want anyone to see the filth on her. She still smelled the scent of the men who molested her all over her body, and it always made her want to puke. One-day, Sylvia was walking by Ms. Geraldine's window when Sharon stuck her head out and told her to come in. Sharon said that she needed to show her something. Syl went through the hallway door that led to Ms. Geraldine's building. When she made it to her door, it was already cracked open. Sharon and Ms. Geraldine were sitting in the living room, and Ms. Geraldine motioned for her to have a seat.

"Syl, Sharon told me that you may need to talk to me. She says that she sees a lot of herself in you. Let me tell you a little something about myself and Sharon. When I first took Sharon under my wing, she was a bruised and battered thirteen-year-old. Her mother allowed her to be molested more than once by men whom she allowed in her home simply because they had drugs to smoke." Ms. Geraldine explained.

Sharon reminisced, "They used to give my mom money to go to the store and get beer. As soon as the door closed, they would pull my clothes off and have their way with me. When my mom would come back and see me crying she would ask, 'What the fuck is wrong with you?' If I tried to tell her that the men hurt me, they would always give her some stupid reason for my crying, and she would slap me and send me to my room to suffer alone. I used to wish that they would just kill me. I imagined that dying would be far better than lying alone after being violated without even your mom to call on. One day after my mom's crack head friends got done with me, they sent me to the store to get cigarettes. I must have worn my hurt like a bright-colored shirt that day because as I walked past Ms. Geraldine's window, she stuck her head out and asked me where I was going. I told her to the store to get cigarettes for my mom. She said, 'Come here for a minute baby, I want you to grab something for me while you are headed that way.' As soon as I walked in, Ms. Geraldine knew exactly what was wrong with me. She said, 'Sharon have they hurt you up there in that house?' I broke down in tears as I replied, 'Yeeeeeeeesssss!' She pulled me in closer and said, 'they will never have a chance to hurt you again baby, never again.' So we are asking you today Sylvia, do you want us to help you? Will you let us make it better?"

Sharon said that she never saw or heard from her mom again after the day Ms. Geraldine pulled her in. The last that she heard, she was in a rehab facility somewhere deep down in Kentucky. As for those crack head men, they both turned up dead in the hood over the course of the following weeks. Ms. Geraldine had some connections through 241 KIDS and managed to get custody of Sharon as well as get a check so that she could have some money for clothes and toiletries. Sharon started to speak again, "Unlike most people who adopted or took in children, she didn't blow the money from the checks. She put me through various martial arts classes and I am a 3rd degree black belt in Aikido as a result. I turned my pain into power. I learned to feel better about what happened to me by developing my mind, body, and soul to a point that I knew I would never be powerless in a situation again. So let me ask you this Syl, when they hurt you, what did you want to do to them?"

Syl answered, "I wanted to kill them... I wanted to shoot them in their penises as well as their faces..."

Sharon said, "Well there you have it. You will master the art of weapons. You will be better at shooting guns than most men. We will get you the best teachers. Let your aim become your therapy and your reputation become your protection. I kick ass Sylvia. There isn't a bitch or nigga that I can't put down if need be. No one plays with me and soon, they will have the same respect for you."

It wasn't long after that conversation that Ms. Geraldine and Sharon introduced her to Bleed. She previously heard of him... Actually, she heard horror stories about the murdering, robbing and torturing that him, Fred, and their flunkies did around the city. Everyone feared them; the police, the big time drug dealers, as well as the street corner dealers. She was fourteen and still had not outgrown her fear of men, but Sharon convinced her that she trusted Bleed with her life. Sharon was confident that she was sending her to someone who could help her overcome her fears and regain her power as a young woman as well as a human being.

Bleed taught her how to aim and shoot a gun when he would go up to his uncle's cabin during hunting season. It was a scary process because one time while shooting a 45 caliber hand gun, her arms jerked back in such a manner that the gun ended up busting her nose. Bleed nor his uncle showed her any sympathy what so ever. They just handed her a rag to wipe her nose and then signaled for her to shoot again. After a few weeks she was shooting guns as if she were born to do so. She went from tagging along on the hunts, to actually hunting herself. Killing animals didn't faze her one bit either; she would always imagine that the blood spilling from the slain animals was the blood of the men who had harmed her as a child. Now Bleed on the other hand, almost had a serial killer approach to killing animals. He liked to just sit and stare at them as the life slowly left their bodies. She often wondered what caused Bleed to be that way but every time she would ask him about his past he would forcefully change the subject.

It wasn't until six months later that Sylvia actually shot a human being. Bleed was in a heated argument with a guy in front of the corner store. She could tell by his mannerisms that he didn't have his gun on him. She heard the guy say, "Well let's go then", signaling that they could just fight to settle the matter but Sylvia wasn't having that. The guy and Bleed squared up. Bleed was actually getting the best of the guy, but just to prove a point, Sylvia hopped out and shot the guy twice in his ass. Everyone looked at her in total disbelief, even Bleed. She stood over the guy as if she was willing to finish him right there if Bleed gave her the word, but he just laughed and said, "Chill shawty, it isn't that serious."

***

Indy wasn't a long ride at all. To Syl, it sounded like this faraway place that took eight hours to get to. However, her and Sharon were at the spa in what seemed to be less than an hour. As they entered the spa, they were greeted by two handsome Hispanic men as well as two Asian women. One of the women motioned for them to follow her to the room where they could get undressed for their massage. This place was beautiful! It was full of soft colors and amazing artwork. The music was calming, a long cry from the noise of those loud mouth whores back on 13th street. They had tiny waterfalls in every corner, beautiful paintings, and elaborate statues. They were shown to a locker room where they were told to strip down as far as they were comfortable and put on robes. The robes were the softest thing that she had ever felt in her life. After getting undressed, they were led to a room with two massage tables where the two Hispanic guys were waiting for them. The massage felt like heaven. Syl thought, this had to be what sex felt like when it wasn't rape. The guy who was doing her massage had very strong hands. When he got to her butt and started to push up on her cheeks, she felt years of pain, hurt, sadness, and stress exit her body. That release of energy was like a sleeping pill because she was soon snoring. When she awoke, the massage was over. She looked over at Sharon's table, and she was slobbering a puddle while sleeping! Sylvia let out a quick laugh and whispered to Sharon, "Wake up; it's over." Sharon arose slowly and said, "Wow Lil Syl that felt like heaven." Syl replied, "I just said the same thing," and they both giggled. There was a knock at the door. Syl said, "Come in." It was one of the Asian women. She gave them both a cup of water and led them into the nail salon where she placed them in some comfy chairs and instructed them to submerge their feet into the steaming blue tub of water. "Oh my God!" Syl whispered to herself. "This is the best feeling ever!" Syl enjoyed every second of the pedicure and manicure, especially the part where they used the cheese grater thing on the bottom of her feet. Next they received facials; getting the blackheads removed from her nose was quite painful, but relaxing none the less. Before leaving the spa, they even got their hair touched up.

It seemed as if they were at the spa forever, but it was only 4 pm. Syl asked Sharon did she hear anything from Bleed because her phone battery was dead. Sharon said, "Yes.

We must hurry to the mall, get clothes, get dressed, and be ready for our men's arrival." The words "our men" threw Sylvia for a loop. Of course, she developed a huge crush on Bleed over the years because he was her savior, but he always played her or looked at her as if she was a little girl. Thinking of Bleed as her real boyfriend caused her to have mixed emotions. Up until today, she hadn't really thought about being someone's real girlfriend, and she definitely hadn't thought about sex. She didn't have any serious sexual desires for Bleed. She used to be in the car with him when he would pick up other girls without feeling the slightest bit of jealousy. Would he expect her to have sex with him tonight? If they did have sex, would he get upset with her for being inexperienced or for not really being into it? All of these things ran through her mind as her and Sharon headed to the mall. Indy's mall was nice. Sharon took her to stores like Cache', Saks, and Nordstrom. She never set foot in stores like these before. These were stores that she always walked by on her way to Foot Locker in the mall back home when she wanted to cop some J's Sharon picked out a cute and fitted dress from Saks for Sylvia. She said it was time for her to show off her curves. They went back to Nordstrom where she hooked her up with some red bottom heels to match her new dress. Although Sylvia was a gym shoe girl, Sharon taught her, along with the other girls in the hood, how to walk in even the tallest of heels. She was strutting for Sharon in six-inch heels at age sixteen. They hurried back to Sybaris to check in and get dressed. Sylvia and Bleed's room was beautiful; fully equipped with a pool and Jacuzzi. The kid in her wanted to jump in the pool so bad, but she didn't want to ruin her hair. She sat on the edge of the bed and thought to herself how Bleed wasn't even sensitive or sentimental. She couldn't believe he did all of this for her.

It seemed like a movie when Bleed and Fred arrived. Sylvia and Sharon were both talking on the phone while peeking out the windows of their rooms when they pulled up. For the first time in her life she looked at Bleed physically; he was tall, maybe around 6'3", and although he wore loose clothing like all of the tougher guys did, you could still see that his body was fit by the way his t-shirt clung to his arms and shoulders. He was blue black, meaning that he was a shade darker than dark skinned, with pretty and polished white teeth. It threw her off that he wasn't dressed up though. He just wore a white tee and some Robin jeans. She hoped that he wasn't rocking that tonight while she was standing there fully dressed, looking as if she was going to the BET Awards. It seemed like it took hours for the men to remove their bags from the car. As soon as she opened the door, Bleed walked straight past her and sat his bags down. She caught a good whiff of his cologne. It was Aventus by Creed, and it was to die for, literally. She knew the smell and the name of the scent because the lady at Nordstrom waved it under her nose earlier trying to sell it to her as a gift for her "man." She said that it was the ultimate gift for a male friend, and now she knew why. Bleed must have bathed before they hit the road because he gave her a quick kiss on the cheek and rushed into the bathroom. It seemed like he was only in there for five minutes but when he came out he looked like one of those mannequins at Nordstrom. He had on a suit; however, it wasn't the type of suit that a man would wear to a funeral, and it was a suit fitted just for him. It made him look like a sexy robot. His dark skin blended perfect with the silvery grey suit. He complimented it with a beautiful pastel purple and light blue tie over a white dress shirt. She didn't think that a guy like him could tie a tie! Where did a nigga that did nothing but cause havoc in the hood learn to tie a tie? He said, "What's up birthday shawty? Stand up and let me look at you." Sylvia stood up and did the girl twirl that Sharon taught all the girls back home to do. He said, "Wow! Unbelievable… you grew up to look just like I imagined you would back when you were only sixteen." He stepped in closer and said, "Kiss me Syl." She wasn't sure if she knew how. He looked her in the eyes and said, "I've waited two years to have you. I could have tried to get it from you when you weren't old enough but I am a man of principle, despite what I do. So I want you tonight. I don't want you to be afraid of the unknown. Don't be fearful of not knowing how to do something because I am here to teach you. Surrender to me, I promise to always love and protect you." He grabbed her gently by the hips and kissed her lips. His kisses became more passionate, and finally she felt her body relax. She opened up her mouth allowing his tongue to touch hers. She felt heat literally going through her entire body as they kissed. It seemed as if he were holding her in the air, suspended in time, while letting his tongue search her mouth as if he was trying to retrieve something. He pushed her away and said, "I knew you were the one from the first day that I laid eyes on you. Even as a young girl I could see the beautiful woman that you would grow to be. I knew that hanging around me and Fred you would learn men: how we think, how we move, and what to expect. This makes me feel comfortable putting everything that I love and value into your hands because you will not react to certain things and situations like typical women do." Sylvia didn't even have to ponder what he meant. She has seen it too many times, even with Sharon and Fred. The second most women think that a man is doing something "wrong", or that he is cheating, they lose it. They start tearing shit up, giving up confidential information, and having their man arrested for bullshit. But he was right, she would never do such things. He said that he hope that he made her 18th birthday the best day of her life so far and promised to make her night even better.

Sylvia still felt like a little girl while sitting at the table with Bleed, Fred, and Sharon but they all went out of their way to make her feel like one of them. When Fred ordered her a drink he told the waitress to bring her the sweetest and most expensive Riesling that they carried because it was her 21st birthday. The waitress was about to ask her for ID but Fred cut her a look so cold and deadly you would have thought that he slapped the poor girl. That was her first time drinking, except for when she took a swig or two of a beer that her mom would leave on the table when she was a kid. Wine smelled like spiced grapes. It didn't have that heavy alcohol smell that wreaked from the winos pores up on the hill.

They ate well, drank more wine, and shared some laughs about the silliness that went on in the hood. When they left the restaurant, Bleed suggested that they ride down to the entertainment district to do the horse and carriage ride like the white people did back home. Bleed and Fred both said that they wouldn't be caught dead riding those things in the city. Sylvia and Sharon both laughed. To Sylvia, an abused little girl, that all sounded like a Cinderella fairytale: so peaceful and fulfilling. The wine that she drank also gave her a sense of calmness.

The carriage ride was wonderful but as the wine started to really kick in, she yearned to be back in their beautiful room. She whispered to Bleed that she was ready to lie down, and he said ok. When they arrived back at the room, there was a box on the bed from Victoria Secrets, and a card attached to it. She opened it, and eighteen $100 dollar bills fell onto the bed. The card itself was beautiful and it read, "Baby girl, I hope to forever have you if God allows me to have a forever. I pray for the day that I can place one hundred $100 dollar bills in your birthday card. $100 for every year of your life that I will be with you. Love Bleed..." Sylvia felt a tear roll down her face. No one ever really told her that they loved her before, not even her mother. She stared at Bleed in awe. She had never seen this side of him and was impressed. The Bleed that she knew was a cold hearted monster. Bleed walked over to the closet to remove his suit. Once he was undressed, he bolted through the door to the pool room and dived in like a little kid. Sylvia was pissed because she was a little curious to see what "her man" looked like naked. He hopped out of the pool and turned on some soft music. The sweet sounds of Miguel's beautiful song *Adorn*, flowed through the surround sound speakers. Sylvia realized that the music was her cue to join him so she quickly got undressed, slipped on the lace lingerie and walked toward him. Her beauty as well as her toned and naked body must have excited Bleed because she saw his lips whisper the words *"damnnnn"* as he looked up at her. She walked over and sat on the edge of the pool. Bleed swam over to where she sat and immediately started kissing on her legs. The combination of the wine, the moment, and the music had her mind all over the place. She didn't know if she should smile or cry. He pulled her legs apart and started nibbling up her inner thighs, and then she felt it… Bleed licked her stuff and she felt her juices gush out onto his tongue. The taste of her wetness drove him wild. He put his arms under her legs and pulled her to him while his tongue searched her hole for more of what she was giving him. She felt herself gush a second time and that made Bleed relax a bit. He gently kissed his way back down her legs and then lifted her right foot out of the water. He licked her right foot from heel to toe, stopping at and nibbling on her big toe. She felt as if she was being shocked with a stun gun. It seemed as if she was about to pee on herself! He did the same thing to her left foot and then he climbed of the water. He held his hand out to help her up. Once she was up, he picked her up. She wrapped her legs around his waist and starting kissing him as she learned to do earlier. Bleed was so strong that his waist, arms, chest, and shoulders were like solid rock, and his shaft that kept bouncing up against her backside was hard like a rock too. He laid her down on the bed and had himself another taste of her, then positioned himself to enter her hole. Sylvia was terrified but not like she was when she was molested as a kid. She was terrified of what was coming next. She never even put so much as a finger in her stuff. She knew that it had to be tight, but Bleed was so gentle with her. He only gave her the tip of it until she started to adjust to his thickness. It felt as if he was going to rip her in two as he began to push deeper and deeper but she wanted it because he wanted it.

She was his now and she wanted nothing more than to make the man happy who brought nothing but joy and security into her life. Tears were running down her face. She wanted it to continue forever; she needed it to be over; she wanted him to stay; she wanted him to stop, and then she heard him grunt. She felt him explode inside of her and it felt good. He collapsed on top of her as if he was exhausted, and with her blood and juices all over him, Bleed drifted off to sleep.

CHAPTER TWO

"THE LIFE OF A HUSTLER"

Cantrell finished his last set of push-ups, slowly rose, and began to pack up his things. He could do push-ups all day long if he had the time. He had been doing sets of 100 since he did a stint in the Department of Youth Services when he was fourteen. Being tall, slim, and light skinned made him a target for the want to be tough guys in DYS, but they quickly learned that Cantrell was really nice with the hands. He was pissed that he was going upstate for drugs that the cops found in his stash house, but felt blessed at the same time because most of it were already gone when they got there. Worst-case scenario, he would receive two, maybe three years for the mid-level trafficking case that he was indicted on. While in the detention center, Cantrell met a brother from Mali who was wrongfully incarcerated on a mistaken identity case. He had to sit for 60 days while his attorneys sorted out the situation. Cantrell found the Malian brother to be very interesting. He gave off a menacing demeanor, yet he seemed so at peace with himself. Surrounded by a bunch of murderers, drug dealers and wild young boys, the brother never seemed to pay anyone any mind. He was completely consumed with his own thoughts. Cantrell noticed that he prayed five times a day, so he figured that he was Muslim. He didn't seem like the violent terrorist type of Muslims that they show you on television though. On the days when there were no activities, the brother would sit in the corner by the window and just read.

One day, Cantrell got up the courage to ask him what it was that he was reading. The brother replied, "I am reading a book called Wisdom for a Peaceful Life by an author named Paulo Corales. When I get done with it, I shall let you read it. You need to read several books my brother, especially where you are going." He continued, "The American prison system isn't designed to straighten out criminals; it is designed to make them more crooked. If you don't want to go in and out of their system, you must focus your mind on the life that you can have once released, not on the things that will go on in there. I can see the confused fire that burns in your eye's brother; they burn without purpose. You long for the center of the storm, the calm part, the part of existence that the Hindu Mystics call nirvana. Fire should be directed. A man should be a master of his own mind, and confusion should not reside within him."

Cantrell didn't fully understand what the brother was saying, but before he could ask for an explanation, he extended his hand and said, "By the way; my name is Maarku." Cantrell shook his hand and responded, "I am Cantrell, Cantrell Solomon." Maarku began to explain what he said to Cantrell. "I see a purposeless life force in you. You have not zeroed in on what it is that you want or need from this life yet. Most criminals remain criminals because they indulge in crime filled lifestyles. They don't even have a purpose for a lot of the crimes that they commit. Black men in America sell their souls for things that they don't need. As long as the white man dangles a thing in front of him, he will sell more drugs, commit more robberies, and kill more of his own kind just to acquire the new thing. Prisons and graves are full of black men simply because the white man has never run out of things to sell them." Those powerful words stuck with Cantrell and while doing the three years that he was sentenced to, he kept his head in a good book and focused on Maarku's life principles. Upon his release; Cantrell tried to patch things up with the mother of his four-year-old daughter, Cannia. She didn't want anything to do with him though. She packed up and moved to Houston with her aunt a while ago and was in a relationship with another man. She did allow him to call and his daughter certainly knew who her daddy was. He promised her that as soon as he was on his feet; he would be down there to visit. Cantrell surely didn't want to go back to hustling. He figured that he would get a trade or work real job until he saved up enough money to start his own lawn care business. He also looked into becoming a barber. He wanted to get his barbers license while he was upstate, but the program lost its funding. Although he had no clue as to what he was going to do with his life, he was determined to live a good and prosperous one like the ones in the books that Maarku gave him to read. He never lost contact with Maarku; they wrote each other his entire bid and Maarku sent him books when he could. He always said he wished he could send money, but he just had too many other responsibilities, and Cantrell respected that. It wasn't long before he ended up working at his mom's brother Roscoe auto repair shop. He was really surprised by the amount of money that he could make in a day helping his uncle fix cars. He was making enough money to pay his uncle rent for a small efficiency apartment, which was in the building that was connected to the shop. He also made it his business to send money every week to Cannia, and although he and her mom had their issues; she made sure Cannia got to spend her money on the things she wanted. She would call him and say, "Daddy I got a new game," or "Daddy I got a new bike." To be honest, her happiness made him focus on the things he had and could do and not all the things the streets had to offer. One-day, Uncle Roscoe told Cantrell the shop would be closed while he went to an appointment. Since they wouldn't be working on any cars, he wanted him to clean the shop from top to bottom. That wasn't a problem for Cantrell. He turned on the radio and proceeded to get busy. By the time he got done cleaning, he realized it was 9pm and Uncle Roscoe still hadn't made it back from his appointment. He figured that he must have gone downtown to the projects and found him some girl to trick with. His uncle didn't have any drug or drinking addictions, but he had no problem blowing his money on a good piece of pussy. His favorite spot was the Fey Apartments on the west side. There was always a young woman who welcomed a couple hundred bucks to service an old man. Cantrell grew extremely tired and hungry from all the cleaning. He was way too tired to cook anything, so he decided that he would just shower, have a bowl of cereal and crash. He heard his phone ring, it was his Aunt Mary Ann. She instructed him to get to the hospital fast. She said that the headache that prompted Roscoe to see the doctor was actually an aneurysm, and they weren't able to get to it in time. Crying, she explained that Roscoe passed away. Cantrell was crushed... he just talked to his uncle that morning. He knew he was complaining of a slight headache, but he never expected this to happen. At that very moment, he saw his life falling apart. He remembered some words of a good friend, "When life kicks you the hardest, the good that you have put into the universe will return to you tenfold. Don't panic in hard times, allow the universe to do its work."

CHAPTER THREE

"LOVE STRUCK"

Riiiiinnnnnnnggggggg... Ameesha heard her alarm sounding. Her hands couldn't stop gripping the sheets. She was caught up in the moment as Dontae's powerful hands forcefully held her thighs open as he gently licked her clitoris with his stiff tongue. Dontae was an expert, or the term that she loved to use for him was "sexpert." It didn't matter if it was with his 12-inch penis, or his slippery tongue, Dontae always managed to control his strokes or licks in a manner that kept her in a euphoric state of mental and sexual confusion. This state lied between the stroke or lick that brought her to the point of climax, and the one that actually made her climax. He had a way of holding her there for minutes on hand without allowing her to cum. When he would finally allow her to release, she felt an explosion... *Boom boom boom!* There was a knock at the door. "Ma, can you turn off that alarm? It's giving me a headache!" "Dammit," Ameesha thought to herself. Her son Lonzo sure had a way of fucking up a wet dream. She reached over to hit the button on her alarm clock realizing that her dream had her clinching the sheets so hard that her hands actually hurt in real life. It's seemed unfair for a woman like Ameesha to only be able to dream of great sex. It would seem that a woman who climbed the accounting ranks at P&T Logistics, worked out every day, and still had her curves just like she did in her early 20s, would be off the market by now. She never imagined being single, unmarried, and unfucked at age of 35, but this was her reality here in Cincinnati. Ameesha graduated valedictorian from St. Ursuline Academy. From there, she went to Miami Oxford where she studied Accounting and Pre Law. In her senior year at Miami, she was offered a mid-level job at P&T which was nothing more than a startup company at the time. She saw its potential to grow, and opportunity for her to grow with it.

**

It was at an office party for employees and potential investors whom she met the father of her son, Alonzo Romell III. Lonzo was raised in Indian Hills and was the son of the famed attorney Alonzo Romell II, who was the defense lawyer for Earl Binder, the EarTron Inc. CEO that was acquitted of murdering his wife back in 2002. Lonzo was 6'1", with a gorgeous dark chocolate complexion. All of the women in the city nicknamed him Morris Chestnut because of his striking resemblance. He was very slender with a muscular build, and had been a star point guard in high school for Summit Country Day. Later, Lonzo attended

Xavier on a basketball scholarship but during his freshman year, he tore his ACL. It was during that down time that he became passionate about law. He realized the genius of his father as an attorney and decided that he wanted to be bigger and better than his dad. He ended up receiving an internship at the prestigious Cohen & Schmeck law firm. He did a lot of the background paralegal work for the city in their lawsuits against Fairview Builders, whom was directly responsible for all the beautiful condos and offices down near the banks area, as well as the mishandling of funds that came along with it. His behind the scenes work on that case led to the conviction of the company's CEO, Lawrence Walters, and earned him fame among all the prominent attorneys in the city. The ladies of Cincinnati loved Lonzo, but he was always known for his unwillingness to commit. He lived a life full of one-night stands and short-lived relationships. You would think an intelligent, sexy, financially stable man who was brought up in a good home would have been forced off of the market, but when Ameesha inquired about his relationship status, he disclosed that he hadn't dated in months.

***

By the end of the event, one would have thought that Ameesha and Lonzo knew each other for years. They exchanged contact information and vowed to see one another sometime within the near future. As Ameesha walked to her car, she wondered if she would really see Lonzo again. Guys like him had a plethora of women, even though they always tried to deny it. By no means did she feel that she was lacking in any way, but she still felt that she just wasn't enough for a guy like Lonzo. He was supposed to be with female doctors, politicians, or other attorneys. She prayed that he would call because he really captured her attention.

The universe had to be listening because the very next day a fruit basket from Edible Arrangements arrived at her desk with a card attached that read: "To the Lovely Ms. Ameesha - There hasn't been a woman since my first childhood crush that has captured my undivided attention the way that you have in just a few short moments. Your conversation was amazing, and you have the body that men crave. When we left each other, I wanted to kiss you and hold you for a brief moment, but I didn't want to be too forward for fear of offending you. I hope that you will make time for me one day soon, I am eager to get past the introductory stage with you so that you will feel comfortable receiving my hugs and kisses. Sincerely Lonzo." Ameesha melted! Never in a million years would she believe that he was thinking about her as much as she had him. She wanted to give him all the kisses and hugs that he desired!

The next day she emailed Lonzo and alerted him that she would be off the upcoming week. He emailed back stating that he would play sick Monday and Tuesday and wanted to meet up. They agreed to meet up at First Watch downtown Monday morning for breakfast, and then go from there.

On Monday morning, Lonzo shot Ameesha a text stating that he would be at First Watch early to do some reading and catch up on a little work before they started their day together. He explained that he would be waiting on her whenever she got there. As she walked into the restaurant, she saw all the movers and shakers of the downtown business district having breakfast. You had the men and women who were just having coffee while reading the Wall Street Journal; the runners; the soccer moms in their spandex running suits sitting around having a bagel and talking about the latest gossip; and you had the young corporate Cincinnatians like herself. She scanned the room for Lonzo and saw him sitting off in a corner like a chocolate Hollywood heartthrob. He must have felt her gaze because he looked up and smiled as she stared. As she walked towards him, his facial expression alerted her that he was taking in her swaying hips as she approached the table. She guessed that she made the right choice by keeping it basic but sexy: flats, tan pencil skirt, white blouse and clear lip gloss. All through high school and college she was known for her killer hips. Even one of her perverted professors once told her that her hips were to die for. Well, this morning she enjoyed watching them kill Lonzo.

He stood, extended his hand, and said, "Good morning lovely!"

"Good morning to you as well sir!" Ameesha replied happily.

During breakfast, they talked about how the city was changing and how the African-American population were spending a large majority of the money. He told her about a plan that he had to take an abandoned portion of the Camp Washington area and turn it into an all-African American entertainment and restaurant district comparable to the one down in the revamped Vine St. area. He also wanted to gain control of the yearly black music festival. He felt that there was no reason for African American promoters to not be able to come together and put on a large-scale concert that could

31

draw patrons from the entire Midwest region. What she loved the most was his plan to have all African American accountants and lawyers enter the middle schools to educate the youth on finance as well as the law. He also wanted African-American business owners to hit the high schools and encourage the youth to work for themselves. She definitely agreed to participate in that program in any way that he needed her. His passion for the people was even more attractive than his outward appearance, and she wanted nothing more than to help him succeed.

"After breakfast and after you tell me all about yourself," he said, "I figure that we can go to the top of the Carew Tower and chill. I've always wanted to do that."

"That's fine with me... I'm just happy to not be spending my vacation in the house." Ameesha expressed.

Ameesha explained to him that she aspired to own a boat. She wanted to ship affordable products from cheaper markets directly to the black community. She explained how she would love to find and ship building materials, as well as furniture to his Black Wall St. project in Camp Washington. She expressed that one of the problems with African-American business are they don't sustain one another. There are too many black retailers and not enough black merchandisers. We need to own the companies that supply our companies. Ameesha felt her panties moisten. These were the types of conversations that were equivalent to foreplay, and she needed more of this in her life.

***

Looking out at the city from atop the Carew Tower

made Ameesha realize how boxed in her little world had been. From up there she saw places in the city that she has never seen. Her parents took her to some of the usual suspect events like: The Taste of Cincinnati, a Bengal or Reds game here and there, and when she turned fourteen, she was allowed to walk around at Newport on the Levee. Her parents focus for her wasn't the adventure, it was strictly education. Everything that they had her involved in as a kid was educational or career based. They left no room for extracurricular activities; she spent the majority of her teenage years locked away in her room. Being confined to her room was where she initially got addicted to porn. She loved everything about porn from the outrageous sizes of the men's penis to the overly stretched holes of the women. When she turned eighteen in October of her senior year and gained just the slightest bit of freedom, she began spending a lot of her time in the XXX stores. She experimented with little dildos and anal plugs, just as she had seen on porn flicks and sexual "How to" tutorials. She watched tutorials on how to deep throat dildos as well as how take them in every hole. A fun Friday night to young Ameesha was one that consisted of some privacy, some lubricant, and some toys. Most of the girls whom she knew at the time were into clitoris stimulators but penetration was her thing, no matter the hole. Over the months, she literally mastered all the tutorials and was handling up to 12-inch dildos with no problem what so ever. It was almost unfair what she did to the boys her age once she started having sex. Even throughout college, Ameesha sprung several boyfriends in the past. She enjoyed watching them go crazy because of what she did to them sexually. Now, she just kept her sexual skills tucked away. She wasn't

33

even sure if she would reveal her full capabilities to her next partner rather it be Lonzo or whoever, because she didn't want to come off as a slut.

***

Their day together was magical... after the Carew Tower, they rode the two-person bike at Sawyer Point and ended the date with dinner at the Brazilian steakhouse. They were both exhausted after dinner, and realizing that both their cars were parked several blocks away near First Watch was rather discouraging. The walk back sealed the deal for her. She felt so at one with Lonzo. He was intelligent, driven, and charismatic that he could have just taken her right there in a downtown alley. She gave him every signal, but being the gentleman that he was, he pulled her close, kissed her briefly, then watched as she got into her car and waved as she pulled off.

The next few weeks with Lonzo were amazing! One week they rode the helicopter at Lunken Airport; the next it was Kings Island. The weekend of August 15th 2006, they attended the Macy's Music Festival as a couple, and ended the night at the Upscale Affair hosted by Hard to Knock Shop. As they entered the Freedom Center through the VIP line, she felt as if they were royalty. She had never been to a club or huge party, but it definitely looked like they were in the place to be. They were rushed to their VIP section by a cute little hostess as the men who were throwing the party walked over and personally greeted Lonzo. Lonzo explained that he and one of the guys used to be work out partners back in college. The music was beyond on point! The DJ kept dropping his name "DJ Skinny Fresh," then he would go back and play nothing but club bangers. Ameesha was feeling it! She never drank before outside of a sip or two of wine, but the bottles of champagne that were waiting on them at their table were enticing. 30 minutes later, she found herself tipsy off of a single glass of Rose' champagne. With the sense of looseness brought on by the champagne, she gained the courage to dance for Lonzo. She eyed a few familiar women doing their two step off in a close corner, so she sashayed her way over to them and joined the party. By the look on his face, she could tell that Lonzo was mesmerized by the way she moved her hips and butt... she even thought that she saw him lick his lips. Being tipsy raised her sense of awareness, and she soon realized that there were thugs and street women in the building. She wasn't feeling that at all. She didn't do hood guys or street people whatsoever. "Who let's these types of people into a party advertised as upscale?" she thought to herself. Her stomach turned and she leaned over to Lonzo and said, "Bae; I don't feel good, can we go?"

As they drove to his place, she noticed that he had an upset look on his face. She waited for a while hoping that it would change but finally asked, "Are you upset that we had to leave the party early?"

"No," he replied, "I'm just a little sad that you got sick on our special night. That's all. I thought that you would finally break down and give me some."

Ameesha had to laugh at his blunt words! She proceeded to say, "Well Lonzo, I have a confession to make... I didn't get sick, I got scared. I saw all the guys with the tatted faces, and heard women talking and arguing as if they were men. I smelled the marijuana on everyone's clothes, and I just felt uncomfortable in that atmosphere. Furthermore, I was ready to be alone with you." Lonzo's eyes lit up with excitement, and he hit the gas a little harder and sped to his place.

Lonzo lived the life of luxury. He stayed in a condo down near Sawyer's Point; complete with a rooftop swimming pool and basketball court. As they entered the lobby, the bellman tipped his hat to greet Lonzo and said hello to them both. As they walked toward the elevators, the bellman yelled out, "You are one lucky man Mr. Romell," causing them both to laugh. Lonzo's condo was immaculate! He said that his mom decorated it for him. It was all decked out in modern art and oriental rugs. He immediately removed his shirt revealing mountains of muscle on a slender frame. It seemed as if the moonlight made his bronze skin shine just like a statue. He glided around the room lighting candles and turned on some soft music. The intoxicating sounds of Playa's hit single, Cheers to You, came from all four corners of the room courtesy of surround sound. Ameesha sat on the edge of the bed anxiously awaiting his touch. He walked over to the bed and pulled her up to him. With her heels still on, and him flat footed, he didn't have to look too far down into her eyes. He kissed her forehead, pulled her close, and whispered in her ear, "over these past few weeks, I have come to love you, but at this moment in time, I just want to fuck you." She instantly got wet as he slid his tongue into her mouth while holding her so tightly that not a single inch of her body could move. He ripped open her blouse and went at her ample breast as if he was a starved animal. His hands were moving so fast that he couldn't get them to work well enough to undo her bra strap. "Oh my god," she thought as he sucked and nibbled on her nipples once he freed her mounds of the bra. He gently bit on her neck, allowing his tongue to sooth each little place that he bit and his tongue felt heavenly. He began to run his tongue and lips back and forth between her shoulder and cheek causing her vagina to drip, then he gently kissed her lips while inserting his finger into her moist spot. "Oohhhhh," she thought to herself. He was making her feel so fucking good. She almost lost control of herself when she felt his tongue gliding inside of her ear as his teeth grazed her earlobe. Her legs wanted to give, but he held her in position as if to torture her with pleasure. This wasn't just lust, this was animal-like lust, and now her body craved him. Her mouth watered for all of him. She reached for his belt buckle, but he pushed her hands away. He pushed her onto the bed and started removing her shorts; he was thirsty to swim in her water. He laid on top of her and inserted himself into her boiling fire. Ameesha secretly laughed at Lonzo; he was only one stroke in, and her wetness was already going to pull everything up out of him. She spread her legs wider to take in his ample rod, then grabbed his ass pulling him deeper into her ocean. Now she was in control, and he was the one being tortured with pleasure, but unlike her, this boy was about to blow. Poor Lonzo; he was only five strokes in when she felt his entire body jerk. He tried to be silent, but just like the ones before him, he sang her song, "Ameeeeessshaaa!" She spread her legs even wider to catch his second explosion and after shaking like he had the chills, Lonzo rolled over with a look of defeat on his face.

Ameesha playfully positioned herself on her knees, with her ass tooted in the air, placing her chin in her hands and stared at her defeated Lonzo. "Don't worry babe, it happens to the best of them. Now go to the bathroom, pull yourself together, and prepare for round two." She said. Lonzo jumped at the opportunity to have a second chance from the woman who just devoured him. He hurried to the bathroom and turned on the shower. He figured a good shower would restore his energy because leaving Ameesha unsatisfied was not an option.

As soon as Ameesha heard Lonzo turn on the shower, she immediately reached for her purse realizing that she left it in his car. She planned on getting herself even wetter with her trusty vibrator and really give Lonzo a splashing. Even with a break to gather himself, she seriously doubted if he would get any further than six strokes the next round. She prided herself on humbling men who were used to pounding on poor helpless vaginas. She decided to throw on her shorts and his T-shirt, and have the bellman get her purse from his car in the parking garage. She grabbed his keys and slipped out of the door.

As she entered the elevator, one of the most handsome white men whom she ever laid eyes upon was exiting. She only got a glimpse of him, but his broad shoulders and stiff military build told her that he had to be a cop or government agent. He wore a nice black suit and looked very official. Upon exiting the elevator, she was surprised to see the bellman standing there as if he was waiting on someone to get off.

"Thank God, I was just coming to find you!"

Ameesha said while slipping him a hundred-dollar bill. "I was wondering if you could retrieve my purse from the back seat of Mr. Romell's car."

"Uhhhh Uhhhhh why sure ma'am. Anything for a guest of Mr. Romell's. He is my favorite resident in the entire building, and he gives nice tips!"

Ameesha laughed as the bellman walked off to retrieve her bag.

"Favorite tenant my ass," the bellman thought to himself as he walked away. He never liked the black snobby fucker. The bellman, whose name was Ryan Garner, never really liked black people, and he definitely didn't like privileged black people who thought that they were better than whites. He almost lost his mind when he found out that Mr. Romell was sleeping with his wife who also worked in the building as the office manager. When the man in the suit approached him a week ago with a tape showing his wife sneaking into Mr. Romell's condo, Ryan wanted to kill her and himself. The man in the suit had a better plan though. All he needed was for the bellman to give him access to the building, a key to Romell's condo, as well as access to the parking garage and promised that Romell would bleed out on the floor of his condo. He also promised that shortly after, Ryan's wife would die in a terrible car accident, and no more than 24 hours after that Ryan would receive a check that would have him set for life. This was a deal that the cowardly Ryan could not refuse.

Just as Ameesha eyed the bellman emerging from the parking elevator, the entire building burst into an uproar!

People were flying off of the elevator screaming, "Someone is shooting on 14!" As the next wave of people exited the elevator, she thought that she heard someone say, "Mr. Romell has been shot!" The bellman raced towards her and said, "Come with me ma'am! Something very terrible has just happened to Mr. Romell! The police are on their way and asked me to get you to safety. I'm going to take you to my wife's office until they arrive." Ameesha was speechless! She followed behind the bellman without saying a single word. Meanwhile, in a federal institution somewhere in California, Lawrence Walters received a message under the door of his prison cell. He opened the small envelope, and read the note which only had a single word written on it: CHECKMATE

The next day, the news reported the murder of Alonzo Romell III as well as a fatal car crash involving Mrs. Karen Garner, both a resident and a trustee at Sawyer's Point condominium complex...

CHAPTER FOUR

"MONEY CAN'T BUY YOU LOVE"

"Man I'm so tired of coming to these bars and clubs. All the women are ratchet and all they want is money!" Darius thought to himself. He hated being single, and hated the Cincinnati dating scene as well. Darius prided himself on being a good man. He believed that outside of a few slip ups here and there; men should give their loyalty to just one woman. His philosophy was that if you found an attractive, non-materialistic career woman with great sex, you should wife her ASAP. Having gone to UC pledging Theta Psi as well as becoming a freemason; Darius knew all the career women of corporate Cincinnati. He dated some while in school as well as some that worked for his company. He was now the CEO of Drake & Bramble Construction, one of the biggest construction companies in the City of Cincinnati. His company overseen the ground breaking and development of

Cincinnati's Freedom Center as well as its Casino. Life was good for Darius, but his love life was in shambles.

***

Darius always had the gift of gab. He could sell himself even when he didn't have anything to sell. In college, he convinced everyone that they just had to have these Black Bonded designer T-shirts. He found a student in the graphics department who printed up some order forms with all the different styles of T-shirts on them and went around taking orders for them when they hadn't even been produced yet. Somehow he managed to pre-sale over $20,000 worth of shirts. He took $1400 of that money and bought a plane ticket to China.

Darius's dad had Chinese business partners. His dad was a software developer. Darius grew up speaking and writing the Mandarin Chinese language. He learned this skill from the wife of his dad's partner. She owned an Asian day care that he attended as a child. He wanted to go to China and find a wholesale supplier for quality plain t-T-shirts that he could get silk screened back home with his Black Bonded moniker. As fate would have it, not only did Darius connect with a supplier, he found a company that did production for startup clothing companies. They even set him up with a silk screener. He explained to the factory manager that he needed the shirts within six weeks. His new-found friend Lee Wong laughed and said, "I only need six days to produce them. It will take longer to ship them to the United States than it would for me to make the garments."

On the flight home, Darius did his math. Out of the

$20,000 that was collected, he would see at the very least $10,000 in profit. "Not bad for a struggling college student," he thought. Through his Chinese connections and his ability to motivate the graphic designers at the university; Darius made a whopping $500,000 in a little over a year, and his big break had yet to come. With a knack for seeing through the eyes of consumers, he came to realize that African Americans would pay for anything that hip hop artist rapped about and celebrities talked about. Darius knew a young local model and singer by the name of Alisha, who now co-starred on the new hit series Love and R&B. He concocted a plan to have Alisha name drop an imaginary brand that he chose to call Waldorf Conceptions. God must have been with him because not only did Alisha agree to do the name drop on the show; she fabricated a story of how she was going to Europe to hunt for a dress designed by the exclusive and elusive brand. She also turned him on to her boyfriend, Burner, the Atlanta rapper who made the hit single Burners on Deck. When Burner dropped his classic verse on the BET freestyle cypher: "I prosper with weapons/I'll teach yo ass a lesson/ got the 45 for protection under my Waldorf Conceptions," the buzz for the brand was crazy. It prompted Darius to mobilize his designers and seamstresses. Whatever he designed he sold and whatever he stocked ran off of the shelves. After a while, Darius grew tired of the fashion industry. Since he was a multimillionaire by the age of twenty-eight, he decided to take a sales position with his dad's friend construction company, Drake & Bramble. Within a year, Darius, being the master salesman whom he was, grew the company astronomically. He got cheaper materials through his Asian connections and pulled in higher revenue. Mr. Drake looked to retire but had only one daughter who enjoyed being a nurse and had absolutely no desire to deal with construction. He turned the company over to Darius, making him CEO. With money came success, and with success came women and Darius dated them all. Since he was rich, his short and pudgy appearance didn't really matter to the ladies. They always made him feel as if he was a tall sexy male model. Over time, he grew tired of entertaining gold digger's and groupies. He also grew tired of the demands of the corporate women whom he dated. He had been in several mock relationships; and none of them were fulfilling. He sexed women from all over the world but what he wanted most was a business-minded woman with some umph and street edge to her. Darius didn't frequent the Cincinnati club scene much at all; however, he always loved to get chicken from Club Celebrities, one of Cincinnati's premier nightclubs. One warm Friday, Darius pulled into the club's parking lot in his 2014convertible Porsche. All eyes were on him. Most guys would have enjoyed moments like this, but he hated unwarranted attention. Darius knew that he was not the most attractive, and that it was the car attracting the attention, not him. He parked his car and hurried past all the people standing in line to get into the club. He made his way straight to the chicken spot. He ordered his usual and from behind him, he heard a woman's voice say, "let me get what he just ordered and put it on his bill." He blew his top on the woman! He went on a wild rant about sack chasers, begging women, ratchet women, etc. The young woman stepped back and said, "Lil nigga, if you would have turned around when I said it, you would have seen that I winked at Larry the cashier! He is my cousin; I get wings from here for free with your stupid and disrespectful ass!" At that moment, Darius felt like a piece of shit. He wrongfully attacked the woman based on a joke. Their food came out at the same time. She took hers and stormed out of the club. Being a man of morals, Darius wanted to at least reconcile with the young woman. He kept asking her to stop walking so fast. He wanted to give her a proper apology, but she just kept walking. He noticed that she was heading towards a brand new 2014 Range Rover. Her license plate read MS. CEO. He felt like a complete fool. He made a mental note of the color of her truck as well as her license plate and swore that he would reconcile with her if they ever crossed paths again.

The next morning, Darius sat in his office still thinking about Ms. CEO. For some reason her sassiness had sparked something in him. He not only wanted to apologize but would also like the opportunity to take her to dinner as well. She didn't look like the type of woman that frequented the places that he did such as Lure, the Day Party, or happy hour at Club 321. She seemed to be from a totally different world. Darius only had one friend from the hood, his partner Jason. Jason was part of his street team back in college when Darius was promoting his clothing line. Jason had written a street novel back then entitled *Why We Are Hood* that received national attention. It also earned him some hefty paychecks. He even sold the movie rights to the book and was now sitting on a decent chunk of change and he was a smart investor. Jason's only problem was that he was still hood. He owned a barbershop down near Lincoln Courts, the neighborhood where he was raised. He was in tune with everything that went on down there. Some even believed that he sold drugs but Darius knew better. He just had dope boy taste with legitimate money. Darius scrolled through his call log and shot Jason a text:

Darius: Bro I need some info on a female.

Jason: I don't know them square ass broads that you love to chase.

Darius: She isn't really square though. For all I know, she could be from down the way.

Jason: Lol! What's the chick's name?

Darius told him that he didn't have a clue. He explained that she was brown skinned with shoulder length hair, kind of tall, and drove a brand new Range Rover that had *Ms. CEO* on the license plate. Jason responded that he didn't have a clue who it was but would keep his eyes and ears open.

Jason immediately put the word out that he was looking for Ms. CEO. He knew that she had to be something serious if Darius was inquiring about her. From what he knew, Darius was still scarred from what that sack chaser Layla did to him.

***

Darius met Layla right when the money from his clothing line had started to pour in. Being new to money, he was new to all the attention that came with it. Layla was a hood chick. The typical dope boy wife type masquerading as an innocent school girl at UC. It was rumored that she was only going to school because all of the tricks and schemes that she ran on street guys had played out. Since everyone was hip to her game, she was forced to turn over a new leaf. Darius met Layla on a Friday at a campus concert. He accidentally stepped on her shoe, a very expensive pair at that.

"Boy! Omg, look what you done!" Layla cried. "These shoes were a gift from my favorite uncle. He would be pissed to know that they are ruined!"

"My bad little lady. I can get them repaired tomorrow." Darius promised. After a few more choice words, Layla calmed down and accepted his apology. They exchanged numbers. "I will black your eye on sight if you don't answer your phone tomorrow." She threatened. Darius instantly fell in love with the spicy young beauty. She was pretty with a homeboy's personality and he could tell that she didn't take any shit. He continued to watch Layla from a distance during the concert. She was there alone and didn't speak or talk to anyone. She was tall with skin like buttermilk. Her hair was long with blonde highlights, sort of like Beyoncé's, and she had slanted Asian type eyes. He looked her up and down when they were up on each other. She seemed to be a woman that kept her essentials together: hair, nails, and toes. He was used to seeing struggling college chicks try to pull themselves together with little to no money but Layla was 100% on point. She didn't look to be struggling at all. He didn't have the courage or the words to just push up on her, so he figured that he would wait to see if she called the next day. If they managed to link up, he would try to get at her on a more personal level.

The next day Darius waited all morning for her to call. He didn't even get out of bed. He figured that he'd rest up until she called, well, if she called. If she did call, he was going to talk her into a full date. He turned on the television and flicked through the channels until he got to ESPN. Before he could settle in to get his morning dose of Sports Center, a text came through on his phone. He leaned over to view the message and it was her:

Layla: Are you ready to get my shoes cleaned chump?

Darius: I am a man of my word so I am more than happy to get them cleaned. Do you want to meet me at the shoe repair shop or do you want me to come and pick you up?

Layla: Pick me up sir! I shouldn't have to burn my gas to fix a shoe that YOU ruined.

Darius: I agree. What time will you be ready?

Layla: Now. I am already up and dressed. Pick me up from 555 McHenry St.

Darius was excited! He danced around the house as he got himself together. He took the fastest shower known to man. He opted to throw on a white tee, an Altatude hoodie and some sweats. He topped his outfit off with some retro J3's. He wondered should he pick her up in his Honda or the Lexus 450 truck? He chose the truck. Since he was a little guy, the least he could do was pull up in a big truck. As he pulled out of the garage of his condo complex, Playa's *Cheers* came through the speakers. *"Cheers to you for giving me a chance, I'll be your angel..."* he sang. The 112 station on Pandora was rocking! As he rode to Layla's crib, he heard 702's hit, *I Still Love You*, as well as 112's *Cupid*. Old school R&B was just what he needed. He would need some smooth game to crack open this tough cookie. He pulled up to the address and called to let her know that he was outside. After about 5 minutes, Layla walked out the door. Looking radiantly beautiful, she had on a tight grey Victoria Secrets PINK sweat suits that made even the smallest of butts appear plump. She was small with perfect curves. The kind that Halle Berry had in the movie Swordfish. She hopped in with the shoes in a plastic bag and immediately tore into him. "Nigga you better hope like hell that they can fix my shoes!"

"I always take my Timbs to D&E shoe repair. Would you like to go there?" he asked.

"My shoes aren't Timbs and all of the ladies that I know go to Elam Shoe repair on Woodburn Ave. I suggest you get there ASAP." She snarled and twisted his ear.

When they pulled up to the shoe repair shop, she hopped out and ran in. Before Darius could even properly park the car she was coming back out of the door. "Mr. Elam said to come back in 45 minutes to an hour." She explained. This was just the hour that he needed to take her out to eat and dig into her mind a bit. "What do you want to do to kill time?" Darius asked. "Lunch," Layla said in her normal snappy tone. He figured he'd ride over to Hyde Park. There was a variety of restaurants over there. Darius noticed that Layla didn't talk much. She would make a few fly comments here and there, but as far as conversation went, she didn't seem like one for conversing. He asked her what restaurant would she like to eat at, and she chose J. Alexander's. As they sat and ate lunch, she began to open up to him a bit. He felt bad for Layla; she had lived a very hard life.

She started with saying, "I apologize if I have been hard on you, I have just been conditioned to act that way. I was molested by my dad, put in foster care, sold for crack by my mom to men who abused me, and have experienced tons of other things that I am ashamed to discuss. I am blessed to be healthy and alive after all that I had been through."

"I agree." Darius said. "Well, I can tell you a little about me. I come from somewhat well to do parents. I never had to deal with the traps and pitfalls of the hood." Darius wanted to shrink down in his seat. He almost felt bad that he didn't have to struggle. When they finished eating and were walking back towards the truck, Layla asked, "Can I have a hug?" she started to cry. Darius was shocked that she viewed him as someone she could release her emotions to. He figured that since they didn't know one another well, she probably felt that he wouldn't judge her. He opened the passenger side door and helped Layla into her seat. "This is a very nice truck. I was so mad about my shoes this morning, I wouldn't have noticed if I were hopping into a Bentley or a hooptie," she said. They both burst out laughing. When they arrived back at the shoe repair shop there was a sign on the door. Layla hopped out to read it then she snatched it off and brought it back to Darius. The note was to inform her that the shoes couldn't be repaired. There were scratches in the suede that showed even after cleaning. The owner closed the shop early and explained that he was sorry for having to leave, but figured that she could get the shoes next week since they were ruined anyway.

Layla had the saddest face ever. She didn't go off like he thought that she would though. She was more upset about not having the shoes when her uncle wanted to brag about what he bought her than not having the shoe itself. Being that her dad molested her, her uncle hated him even though he was his brother. He took pride in stepping up to the plate and caring for his niece. He loved to brag to the family about what he did for her and would say things like, "Layla show them the necklace and purse that Unc got you."

Darius felt horrible. He stepped up and did what he thought was only right.

"Please allow me to replace the shoe," he begged.

Layla screamed, "Those shoes cost $1600 dollars, not to mention they are a hot commodity! I doubt if Saks even still has them."

"Is there an alternative?" Darius asked, still trying to find a way to fix the situation.

"Well... Maybe you could buy another Louboutin shoe and if Unc ask, I could tell him that the ones he bought me had a defect and I had to send them back." said Layla.

"No problem," Darius smiled and headed toward Saks.

There was never anywhere to park, so he handed her his American Express card and told her to get whichever pair that she saw fit. Besides, his sole purpose for waking up this morning was to make this shoe situation right with Layla. She returned to the truck about 15 minutes later. She handed him the card and the receipt; the shoe was $950 dollars. Layla explained that although the ones he ruined cost $1600, she actually liked the new ones better. With Layla happy, Darius felt off the hook for the extra $650. It wasn't that he wouldn't have paid it, but he was glad that he didn't have to.

Darius didn't want to drop Layla off but he realized that they weren't dating. He just didn't feel comfortable asking for more of her time. He figured if she liked him she would ask to see him again. Besides, manning up and replacing the shoe should have scored him some extra brownie points. They pulled up to her house. Layla said, "By the way, I'm not mad anymore about my shoes. You seem to be a nice man. You will make some lucky woman very happy one day." She gave him a quick kiss on the cheek and hopped out the truck before he could say a word.

Darius stomach began to knot up. He couldn't understand what happened. She seemed to like him yet she played him so neutral. She was not impressed by his car, money etc. He wasn't shallow, but he did feel that maybe he deserved some sort of recognition. In an era full of bullshit black men, he wasn't one of them. It crushed him to be played so irrelevant but she did say that he would make some lucky woman happy. He rode off confused. *"Why wouldn't she allow me the opportunity to make her happy?"* He thought. His self-esteem was diminishing as he headed back down Harrison Avenue. He thought about getting a gym membership so he could lose a few pounds. He even contemplated buying a flashier car or some jewelry like the street guys. He decided to grab his favorite milkshake from McDonalds, the vanilla one. He sat in the lot reflecting on life, Layla, and what he had to do to get her. He had concluded in his mind that he wanted her and would do just about anything to have her.

Halfway through his milkshake his phone began to ring. It was Layla. "Darius can you please do me a favor? I need a ride right now! Can you come back and get me?"

Darius hurried back up the Harrison Avenue hill. One of Layla's cousins had stolen her rent money out of her purse and they were in the house about to fight. She needed a ride because her car wasn't there. Darius pulled up to the house and could hear all of the screaming and hollering coming from the house. He could even see some of the commotion through the screen door. He decided that it was best to just blow his horn. Layla stormed out towards his truck. A chick that he assumed was her cousin came out on the porch screaming, "Bitch don't nobody need to steal from you! I gets to the cash, you weak broke bitch!" Layla hopped into the passenger seat and barked, "Pull off!" As he was driving, Layla began to shake and cry. "This has to be the worst weekend ever! First my shoes got ruined, then this bitch steals my rent money out of my purse. I started to take my purse with me but I didn't think that we would be gone that long but I guess it was too long! My purse must have looked tempting to that young, dumb bitch. It just seems like I can't catch a break. I'm just trying to go to school and be better than the people in my family. It seems like my family are the ones that keep pulling me down. I just had to give up my apartment so I'm staying there with my aunt and my cousin. Being that we are all adults, we take turns paying the rent in full once every three months. I was going to give that money to my aunt when she got home from work. My cousin that stole it is her daughter. My aunt would put me out before she believed that my cousin was a thief."

Darius felt horrible. "Is there anything that I can do?" he asked. Being that this unfortunate chain of events was his fault, he felt it was only right to offer help.

"No. You have done enough." She expressed. "I am not the type of woman to ask a man for anything, especially a man that is not my boyfriend or husband. Thank you for coming to get me out of the house though. I needed to think and there was no thinking in that chaotic house. I apologize for getting you caught up in all of this bullshit. I just can't figure out why I have so much bad luck! It's like it follows me around." Layla said in a sad tone. "Darius, you are a good hearted person and a standup guy. I would love to date or be with a guy like you. Guys like you are a breath of fresh air but I'm not even dateable. I would never want this black cloud to be hanging over your head too." She explained.

"When two people like one another, they fight battles together. I am going to help you get a grip on things. Where is your aunt?" he asked.

"She is at work." Layla replied.

"Let's take her the rent money and sweep all of this under the rug. You don't even have to tell your aunt that your cousin stole from you. We will do that and then start off fresh." Darius offered, hoping that this would please her.

Layla said, "You have done enough. I couldn't expect you to do that. You don't owe me anything."

Darius replied, "Technically I do. I ruined a pair of $1600 dollar shoes and the ones that you bought to replace them only cost $950. I feel that I still owe $650 and the additional $100 isn't much to pay either for the inconvenience that I have caused you. Layla gave him the address to her aunt's job. He punched it into his navigation system and they went there to give her aunt a check for the rent.

After having dinner with Layla that evening, they made plans to see each other later on in the week. Darius never would have imagined that this would be the last time that he saw or heard from Layla. He called her phone repeatedly after that day and not one single time did she ever pick up. One day, word got back to him through Jason of how Layla was on Facebook bragging about how she had played him like a fool. Some girl told Jason that Layla ran it down; how she paid Mr. Elam $50 dollars to close the shop early and to post a note on the door saying that the shoe couldn't be repaired. She allegedly referred to Darius as a cock lick and bragged about how she got him out of $750 and a pair of $950 shoes.

CHAPTER FIVE

"MS. MADE BITCH"

"Uggghhh, this Bluetooth takes long as fuck to connect!" Morgan couldn't wait for her phone to pair so she could call her friend Ash. "About time!" Morgan yelled when the Bluetooth made the *connected* sound. She scrolled through her contacts until she got to the name Ashley, and hit the call button. After three rings that seemed like they took forever, Ash answered. "What's up girlie?"

Morgan went in, "Girl, you won't believe what just happened to me! I'm in line at the chicken place in Celebrities and I'm standing behind this short guy who was placing an order. I wink at my cousin Larry, the cashier, and then tell him to put my order on the short guy in front of me bill. Before I could even laugh he flips completely out! He gets to talking about how he is tired of sack chasing and begging ass women! Right then it was obvious to me that he had no clue who I was!"

Ash burst out laughing, "Woooooowwwwww! If I were you, I would have told that lame that I owned Club Fire as well as prime real estate! The last thing that I needed from a man was three wings and medium fry money."

"Right girl! Not to mention that I have a brother with money, who is hell bent on keeping me in a position to never need a man. My brother hates it when I meet men, especially here in the city. He doesn't think that any of the men here are worthy of me. He said that working dudes are crazy and possessive, and hustlers are just dogs. Let's not get on broke dudes, they are just out of the question. With all of his stipulations and expectations, one day I found myself on a date with my vibrator! I didn't have anyone to go to the movies with, so I politely threw Walter, my vibrator, in my purse and went to see the movie with him. I figured if I couldn't be with the one that I'm loving, I could be with the one that I'm fucking!" screamed Morgan. She was on a roll tonight!

Ashley start laughing, "You went on a date with a handsome vibrator? Hahahahahaha!"

"I know right, it sucks to be me... it sucks to be me." Morgan said shamefully.

***

Morgan never expected to be without a husband at this point in her life. Better yet, she never expected to be without a boyfriend but here she was. Being the daughter of Big Prez and growing up in the notorious 4 section of Avondale came with a lot of seclusion and secrecy. Her dad allowed her brother to run the streets and have fun. He felt that if anything went down, Lil Prez could protect himself. But not her, she had to either stay in the house or go hangout somewhere in the suburbs with her white friends from school. Boys were out of the question too. If one of the Rockdale boys even caught a glimpse of her, her dad and her brother were always there to run them off. She was twenty-eight years old now and may as well still been a virgin. She hadn't seen a real penis since God knows when. Her senior year in high school, she went to the prom with her boyfriend Paul Manly. Afterward, they pleasured each other with oral sex. He tried to penetrate, but he couldn't manage to get it in so they just cuddled and talked all night. Their dealings fizzled after prom night and he went off to basketball camp that summer and she got thrust into adulthood by the passing of her father. Her dad suddenly got an infection in his bloodstream due to a bullet that had been lodged in his leg for over 15 years. Once he passed, she was forced to learn all about the bar business from her Aunt Jess as well as how to manage the rental properties that he had left her. Her brother found over 50 kilos of dope that her father had yet to move before he died. He allowed everything that their father had to go to Morgan so she was pretty much set for life as long as she managed things properly. Prez took to the streets really hard. It was as if he wanted to live up to their father's rep instead of living off of what he had built.

Financially set and love life in shambles was the story of her life. In all honesty, she had been so caught up in life that she didn't even think about sex, especially after what happened with Jake when she was twenty-one. Jake was a young, white, handsome bartender at Dave & Buster's entertainment complex. One of Morgan's favorite things to do when she was bored was to go and play a few games and then have a big ole sundae at the bar. Jake always had her sundae perfectly made just for her with extra fudge and whipped cream. Till this day, she didn't know how it happened or why it happened but one particular Saturday night, she ended up giving her virginity to Jake. Maybe it was a way to rebel against her overbearing brother Prez who literally hated any man that tried to talk to her or maybe she was just open and feeling adventurous. Whatever Jake said to her that night while she ate her chocolate chip sundae worked. If sugar could cause a person to be intoxicated she would have said that she was just drunk, but hey, shit happens. She recalled giving Jake a blowjob, something that she learned to do oh so well while hanging around the white girls back in private school. Some of them used to play a game called, "Who can deep throat the banana". Needless to say, she became highly skilled in the area of giving BJ's. She reminisced about Jake sucking her soul out of her through her vagina. She remembered him getting on top of her and how she braced herself for the pain. She had heard since high school how painful that it was for a girl to get her virginity taken, but she felt nothing. Jake took a couple of pumps, shook a little, rolled over, and starting snoring. She eased out of the bed once he was sound asleep. She checked the sheets for blood, but there was none. The only thing in the bed was Jake's used condom, full of semen. She reached down to grab her clothes and slid into the restroom to get dressed. She left Jake's apartment and never looked back. She never even went to Dave & Buster's again. She just tried to block the entire incident from her mind.

***

That had been over 5 years ago, and to be honest, she hadn't thought about men since. She had a little fling here and there with white guys that wouldn't raise her brother's eyebrow, but she still hadn't found fulfillment. People always saw how she looked, was built, her style and her fly mouth and automatically assumed that she was about that life. Truth be told, she was just a private school nerd/white girl with black skin who merely picked up on the slang and style of the streets because she had a brother who was *that nigga* according to the hood. Being around him at times is where she got her edginess from. She was built like a stripper simply by genetics. Her mom was a dancer back in the 80's in Atlanta Georgia. It was in a strip club that her mom met her father, Big Prez. Her mom always told her when she was thin that she would fill out and boy was she right. Nowadays, she turned heads wherever she went. She was tall and thick with just enough ass and tits to make a man turn his head; even while walking with his girl in the mall. Speaking of the mall, she thought to herself, she needed to get there ASAP. Prez was letting her and Ash go to the BET awards in Atlanta with him in a few weeks. She needed a vacation and for all intents and purposes. She wanted some manly attention, even if it wasn't sex, she just wanted to hang out at the hotel or go out to eat with some sexy and fun guys. Hopefully Atlanta could provide that for her and Ash when they got there.

CHAPTER SIX

"WHAT'S UNDERSTOOD DOESN'T NEED TO BE EXPLAINED"

Sylvia struggled with people thinking or believing that she was skept, or that she robbed like Bleed and Fred did. Because of that, she didn't have a lot of female friends. Their boyfriends, baby daddies, and brothers were all afraid of her. After being around Bleed and Fred since she was fourteen, she gravitated towards men anyways when it came to friendship. A lot of the confused emotions and cattiness that women her age displayed didn't reside in her. She viewed things through the logic of males and not through emotion like most women do. The only time that she felt the slightest bit of emotion was when she was around Bleed. From jump, Bleed told Sylvia that he would care for her and protect her, and he did just that. At just eighteen, he had got her a nice 2500 square foot apartment in Mt Lookout. It was close enough to, but far enough away from the city to where she would be safe and comfortable. He made sure that she finished school. She received her diploma from Taft High school. He, Fred, Sharon, and Ms. Geraldine all attended her graduation. He knew that she wasn't really into school all like that so he never pushed her to attend college. What he did insist upon was that she get some sort of trade so that she could work or start a business if anything ever happened to him. This prompted Sylvia to enroll in Great Oaks for Web and Graphic Design. She completed their program in no time. She wasn't pressed for money, so she didn't work. Bleed said that there were several small turf wars going on throughout the city. Bodies were dropping like crazy, including women and children. He said that her working somewhere was too stationary and anyone who knew where she was working would have an advantage over him. Coming from a street background, she knew this all to be true. Bleed paid all of her bills and when he would hit big licks, he would give her 15% to put into her own bank account. As far as spending money went, he would randomly drop pass her house and leave a wad of cash on the kitchen counter for her to blow. Coming from where Sylvia came from, the way that she was living today was the Life. Her closet was full of brand new clothes and all of the boosters had her number on speed dial. She was so in with the boosters that if they had something that she liked, they would just drop it off to Ms. Geraldine and get their money from her later. Shoes, bags, jewelry, you name it she had it. Bleed loved to go to Chicago, Detroit, and New York to shop, being that there weren't many places within the city where he could shop and feel safe. He learned his lesson fast when one day he was in Shoe Lane over on Hopple Street purchasing some new sneakers.

The chick that worked the register called her brother L in which Bleed had robbed previously. Unbeknownst to Bleed, L and his goons were waiting outside for him. The only thing that saved him was that a chick who knew Syl from the hood just so happen to peep the set up going down and text her. Syl and Sharon were at Ms. Geraldine's when she received the text. She instructed Bleed to play it off and to keep looking at or trying on shoes. She told Sharon to throw on some white pants, a thong, and her tallest pair of heels. They pulled up to the barbershop across from the shoe store. She let Sharon out and told her to walk into the store. All of the men's eyes followed Sharon's huge behind and her swaying hips. Just like clockwork, they took the bait. Sylvia could see the guys all pointing at Sharon, so she made her move. She pulled off as if she was going to exit the lot, driving directly past the car full of goons. She let the 40 caliber go right through their front windshield. She seen at least two of her bullets hit the driver and the guy in the passenger seat directly in the face. If there wasn't so many witnesses, she would have hopped out and made sure that everyone in the car was dead just like Bleed had taught her. Instead she slid off just as smooth as she slid in. No one realized what had happened until she was long gone. Bleed said that he and Sharon peeped a girl get nervous after everyone heard the shots. She was the only one texting instead of trying to see what happened. Sharon walked towards the girl and said, "Bitch I ain't got to steal out of here, you got me fucked up!" and commenced to wailing and kicking the girl. Bleed and Sharon slid off before the police came. Everyone got what they deserved. People had to learn the hard way that Syl would kill for her Bleed.

CHAPTER SEVEN

"THE TURN UP"

"Bruh, there goes shorty that I have been trying to catch back in the city! I'm about to invite her into our booth." Darius exclaimed.

"No the fuck you aren't!" Jason replied. "You have no game at all. If she is here in ATL, obviously she has talked to some guy from the city or maybe even from out of town that has invited her to be in his booth. Be more observant. She already has on a VIP wrist band, she isn't walking through looking to get pulled into a random booth. She is looking for the booth that she has already planned to be in. Her name is Morgan. I don't know her but I came across her page on Instagram once. She does some sort of promotions back in the city."

Darius had to admit that Jason was right. Hopping out of the booth and popping some weak game would not impress a woman like Morgan. Women like her get pursued by all of the street guys back in the city as well as the corporate guys. Even though he had money, he wasn't raised to show his money. Therefore, Darius knew that he wasn't a woman like Morgan's first choice. They tend to have their eyes and ears open for the more popular guys back in Cincinnati.

"Man look," Jason said while pointing and laughing at the same time. "She is headed for Prez and Spade's booth. I don't know why I'm telling your lame ass that, you wouldn't know Prez and Spade from a can of paint. Those cats are from Avondale. They are the enforcers for some white guys out in Delhi that are getting a lot of money. Word is, they are the link between the white guys that got it in wholesale and the black guys who need it in the hood. Prez is a wild nigga. He is what they call a shooter in the hood. When shit pops off, he is the first to shoot. Now his partner Spade on the other hand is a pretty boy. He is the diplomat. He handles all of the business and is also the guy that gets the women. Prez just scores because Spade gets him his shots, you feel me? Prez is also known for paying big money to fuck, so any woman who has a band on to get in their both will definitely be pushing up on those cats heavy. They know if they score they will get to tear down Lenox mall tomorrow afternoon."

Darius completely understood what Jason was saying. These guys that Morgan was around were heavy hitters back home. She was more than likely where she wanted to be so he might as well get her out of his system. Realizing this ruined the night for Darius. He had only come down to the Awards Weekend because he didn't frequent the spots back home that Morgan would probably hang out at.

***

When Darius saw Morgan again after the chicken spot incident at Nordstrom in Kenwood Mall, he had fallen completely in love. He was afraid to approach her. She looked like perfection and as if she required it as well. The woman was drop dead gorgeous; light caramel complexion, long jet black hair that hung down her back and seemed to be natural, and a medium sized but perfectly round butt. Her best quality was her eyes though. She had those same slanted Asian eyes like the rapper Foxy Brown had. It gave her a very exotic appearance. While Darius was waiting to get a battery put in his watch at the mall, he noticed something about this woman that alarmed him. She purchased a $350 dollar Michael Kors watch with all $5 dollar bills. Seeing that large dirty wad of cash made Darius wonder if she was a stripper or was her boyfriend a drug dealer? Either way, the woman was undeniably beautiful and Darius had to have her in some way, shape or form. Her phone rang as she waited to get her new watch sized. He overheard her telling a girlfriend that she was at Nordstrom purchasing a watch and some shoes for the big party that was going down at the Flex Room during the awards weekend. Aaron Broadnax, the local boxing champ from Cincinnati, was celebrating his birthday there and it was rumored that any woman with a Cincinnati ID could drink for free all night courtesy of him. She sounded excited about it and Darius wanted to be there too just to see this woman again. Most men would have tried to approach her at the mall right then, but his confidence wasn't set up like that. His past experiences with women always caused him to question if he was attractive or desirable enough to just walk up and talk to a woman that he liked. Standing 5'2"as a man didn't help either.

Darius hated clubs and had never been to a crowded event that consisted of drugs and liquor. Club events wasn't his thing at all. Darius was afraid of guns, thugs, fights, and all of the things that came with liquor and black people. He decided to call his boy Jason. Jason always tried to keep Darius away from street women, especially after Shawna *ran up a check* on him just a year ago. And let's not forget about Layla who played him as well. Darius fell for all of the street chick schemes that even the dumbest of hustlers wouldn't have gone for. A skept woman and an insecure man with a big heart and deep pockets was always a recipe for disaster. He knew that if he wanted to go to this event and pursue this woman without getting *took up top*, he would need Jason there with him every step of the way. Jason agreed to go under one condition. He said that for once in his life Darius had to blow some money and live little. He insisted that they buy Rolex watches when they got there as well as do some high end shopping. Darius didn't debate with him. For Ms. CEO, he was willing to go with the flow and whatever came with it.

Darius shook from his thoughts when he felt Jason shake his arm, "D, look, for some reason they are moving everyone from Prez's booth on the stage to the vacant one across from us. Good lawd, look at that ass and perky tits on baby girl that you are stalking."

Darius was awe struck. Morgan stood up at the front edge of the booth and began to dance to Fab's *You Make Me Better*. Her skirt was having a hard time containing her hips. Darius truly admired the way that she danced; he concluded that she couldn't be a stripper. The other women in the booth were throwing it around extra hard and she was doing the minimum amount of shaking yet she gave off a maximum amount of sexy. As he stared, Darius noticed that the Prez guy offered Morgan an entire bottle of Bellaire champagne. She accepted the bottle. He went back and sat next to a woman that didn't look anywhere near as good as Morgan. She must have felt Darius staring because she glanced up at him and gave him the "What the fuck are you looking at" face. Darius was pissed, he decided to have a drink to get his mind off of her. Jason was outside the booth offering booth worthy women drinks and a seat. None of the women that obliged were of the caliber of the women in Prez's booth. Darius felt defeated, although the women in his booth were shaking ass and being friendly. He just didn't want to be there. Jason sat down next to Darius and said, "You really want that chick huh bruh?" Darius shook his head to imply yes. "How much cash did you bring?" Jason asked.

Darius said, "$10,000 dollars."

"Give me $4,000." Jason said.

Darius counted out forty $100 dollar bills and handed them to Jason. Darius asked if he was going to offer Morgan the $4,000 to sleep with him? Jason said, "No fool! Them niggas got money too! You don't fight money with money, you fight money with game." At that point Darius was lost so he just took a drink and watched the women in his own booth turn up as they drank. He decided that he wouldn't even glance back at Morgan's booth.

Jason exited the booth with the four grand locked and

loaded. He scoured the club for a bad chick or a group of bad chicks that weren't in anyone else's booth. He looked for every bit of 15 minutes and then lucked up. Two of the baddest women that he had ever seen in his life; one light skinned, one dark; both walked out of the restroom area looking as if they had just walked on to a movie set. These women were naturally beautiful too. They weren't the overly made up and plastic type, they were just two bad built and fly dressed women with no filter. Jason decided to nickname them Salt & Pepper. He noticed that neither had a wristband meaning that they didn't have a designated area to go to. He stepped to Pepper and said, "I know you are about to say something fly to reject me but I am coming to ask you ladies for a favor that could benefit us all. It's nothing sexual and it doesn't involve exchanging numbers. Shit, it doesn't even involve knowing each other's names."

Salt frowned with disgust but then said, "What the fuck is it?"

Jason pulled out the $4,000 and said, "I'm waiting on my people to come in so I need to walk to the front. The waitress for our both over there (he pointed towards the booth) is taking too long and we need bottles. Would you ladies mind waiting in line and grabbing me a case of Bellaire?"

Pepper replied, "A whole case?"

Jason said, "Yeah, a case".

Salt said, "So you are going to trust us with your $4,000 and you don't even know us?"

Jason replied, "Any worthwhile friendship or relationship begins with trust, and ends with distrust; I am trusting you ladies to be my new friends or you can leave the club with my money and become an enemy. We may or may not ever cross paths again, but if we do, you can be sure that you won't like me being your enemy."

Both chicks laughed and said in unison, "We will see you at the booth homie." They laughed louder as they walked towards the bar. Jason took a second to take the two women in. They both had on red bottoms, female Rolex's, and Pepper was carrying a bag that Jason seen in the Rob Report magazine. He couldn't remember the name of the bag but it cost every bit of $20,000 dollars. These women knew someone with some serious money. Just then, Jason realized that he didn't tell the women that Darius was in the booth. Jason trotted up behind the ladies and told them a story about how his home boy Darius was in the booth depressed because his ex was in the booth across from theirs with a guy. He told the ladies that when she saw them walk over there though, she would be the one that gets jealous. The ladies both laughed and Salt said, "I love making movies for hoes. Trust me, she will know that he is in the building by the time that I'm done." Jason walked off with confidence. He had set the chessboard into play for his man Darius to win.

Jason watched the ladies from afar, and just like he thought, the bartenders went into a frenzy over the case order. Probably apologizing for the slow service to the booth and promising that the owner of the club himself as well as his top waitresses would deliver the bottles personally. Jason watched as they made their way towards the booth. He saw the excited look that Darius had when he seen them. He also saw the salty looks on the faces of the other women that were already in the booth. Darius couldn't believe his eyes. He was staring at dark and light skinned perfection. These two women were the most beautiful and well put together women that he had ever seen. One was a few shades darker than high yellow, with clear and beautiful skin, seemingly no make-up, natural hair, and a huge derriere that didn't even seem to go with her petite waist and small but perky tits. She looked like a cuter version of Christina Malian in the face. The dark skinned one was pitch black. She had to be native African. She had full lips and beautiful eyes. She was a tad bit taller than her friend, a bit slimmer but just as curvy. She had a stronger sex appeal though, sort of like the character Chiquita from the movie Belly. Both women looked like a lot of money! Darius's mouth dropped when they both said, "Hi Darius." He began to stutter, "uhhhh uhhhh uhhhh du du du do I know you ladies?" Pepper said, "We are your guardian angels," and kissed his cheek. Even though Darius knew that she was joking, he kind of believed them. Both women stood up in the booth and turned to face Morgan and her girls in Prez's booth. A subliminal dance contest started between the women in both booths when Bobby Shmurda's smash hit *Hot Nigga* came on. Jason was still off in the cut working his magic. He couldn't remember Morgan's Instagram name, but he knew that everyone from Cincinnati were scouring their newsfeed trying to see who else was in the club, what they were doing, and who they were with. Jason snapped a pic and uploaded it. Their booth looked turned up and he added the caption, "Me and my homie low key D about to turn up in the Flex Room." At the same time, he watched as the entourage of waitresses walked towards their booth with 12 bottles of Bellaire complete with sparklers and fancy gold champagne flutes. Jason gave himself a pat on the back, he had just made a movie. By the time he walked back to the booth and checked his phone, the pic that he uploaded had received 70 likes. He checked the people who liked the pic and there she was, Morg_badass513. Now that he knew they had her attention, he sat back and allowed the ladies to work their magic.

Morgan kept staring at Darius. Having had a father and a brother from streets, she had a photographic memory of people and places. Darius was the guy from Nordstrom a few weeks back that kept eye fucking her. He was creeping her the hell out that day. He looked like he wanted to eat her ass right there in the mall. He was also the little asshole that fronted on her in the chicken spot. In his defense though, unlike most guys like him, he didn't waste his time or breathe trying to score with a corny pick up line. He didn't say a thing to her. *"Little arrogant fucker,"* she thought to herself. He was a little too short for her taste. A lot shorter than her, but he looked strong as fuck. He looked like he could and would manhandle a chick in the bedroom. The case of Bellaire topped with the two blinged out model chicks that were all over him told her that his short ass had some money. It was obvious that he was the baller because she knew the guy Jason who was with him only cut hair. His name never came up in the money conversations but he still managed to screw a lot of women around the city. Morgan continued to dance as if she wasn't paying their booth any mind, however she couldn't shake the sight of that dark skinned hoe in Jason's booth. She was bad. Game recognized game and even the polish on her toes where shining like they were painted with diamond paint. She wondered were those two from Cincinnati, but then she thought, "Nah. Most Cincy chicks can sometimes get over excited when money is in the building. They would be over there boppin hard. The hoes over there were just chilling how men chill, those girls are a little bit more polished than the typical chicks back home."

Pepper whispered to Darius, "The dark cute girl in that booth over there wants you."

"How did you conclude that?" he asked.

She said, "I told you I am your guardian angel. I'm watching who is watching you. Shit, she is watching you and me. She is good though, most bitches would be openly hating by now and trying to dance all hard. She has some polish. She is holding her composure, but when she looked down and seen this Rolex Gold nail polish on my toes, even from a distance, it broke her back. It's made to shine like a diamond encrusted Rolex watch!" She told Darius to walk to the bathroom and she guaranteed that the girl would follow behind him.

Darius did as she instructed. He exited the booth and walked towards the bathroom. He didn't want to look back to see if Morgan was following so he figured that he would glance back when he took the three little steps up to the bathroom platform. Sure enough, when he got his chance to glance, Morgan was in tow. When Darius exited the bathroom Morgan was right there. She said, "I knew that was you! You were the creep on my ass a few weeks ago in Nordstrom!" Darius decided to play the "too polished" role that he had seen Jason play before. He replied, "Who me?

Why would I be on your ass?"

She snapped back, "I don't know, but your ass kept staring at me at the watch counter. I haven't forgotten about when you flexed on me in the chicken spot either!"

Darius acted as if he was deep in thought and then said, "Ohhhhh, I thought that was you. But then I figured that I could have the wrong person so I left it alone. Glad to see you here and I apologize for my rant at the wing spot. I was having a bad day. Well I hope that you are having a good time while you are here, have a nice evening. By the way, I'm Darius. Darius Thompson. And you are?"

"Oh, my name is Morgan. Morgan Dickson."

Morgan felt a bit let down but she refused to show it. She assumed that he would jump at the opportunity to get at her being that he was at her hard in Nordstrom. He actually acted bothered by her just now. He said, "Have a nice evening", and walk away? Who the fuck did he think that he was? Morgan was consumed with the thought that those two out of town heifers knew something that she didn't. She felt that this guy must be a hidden gem back home because those bitches were bad and they were on him heavy. They looked as if they knew how to pick them. Morgan was not about to let some out of town broads have a man from her city. She decided to take him by force. *"If these out of town hoes still wanted parts, they would have to share!"* she thought. Yeah, they can come in town. They can even spend some of his money but they would have to share with her. Morgan didn't mind sharing a good man. So many of her friends and colleagues stressed over the bad ones that they had all to themselves.

She figured if she was going to get fucked over anyway, it would be by a man with some promise. When her brother schooled her on men he would always say, "Sis think about your future children as well as your current family when you choose a man. Bring a man into our family that is about something. One that I can build with and who can help our family strive as a whole. Don't pick a man for simple minded selfish reasons like he won't cheat. I know that no woman wants to get cheated on, but shit, if cheating is going to occur anyway let it be by a man that is worth something to you; not some bum ass loser." She tried preaching Prez's philosophy to her friends. They weren't having or hearing it, yet they all stayed on that hamster wheel of, "He cheated and I'm leaving." They couldn't tell if they were coming or going.

If those women in his booth were from out of town, she felt that she had the advantage because she lived in his city. She was confident enough in herself that she knew if she was the one he spent the bulk of his time with then he would gravitate towards her. Once he realized that she wasn't one of those sack chasing whores and didn't need a single penny from him, he would fall in love.

Darius walked away sweating bullets. It took everything in him not to rip Morgan's clothes off and put his tongue in places that she didn't even know a tongue could go right in the club. She was a stunning beauty with a cool around the way girl vibe. She didn't even come across as arrogant as he would have thought. He was now convinced that he owed Jason one because even as he walked away, he felt that Morgan was going to be on his ass. Darius made it back to the booth. Jason was already smiling, "Praise me brother; call me King. She was looking at you like you were *steak* as you walked off." Salt as well as Pepper said bow to the queens because your beauty is walking directly towards our booth". Everyone played it off in unison as Morgan walked up the steps and into the booth and said, "Isn't it common practice when you see a woman from your own city to offer her a drink and a seat in your booth sir? Oh let me guess, you bosses are too good for city women and you only kick it with out of town women, right? Oh, by the way ladies, you killed it tonight! That Rolex Gold nail polish with the matching Rolex that you are rocking is to die for. If you two were from Cincinnati, I would be hating on both of you big time but being that I'm the flyest thing that my city has to offer, I don't feel threatened!" Morgan and the ladies burst out laughing "Actually, I need both of your numbers for fashion tips." Salt & Pepper loved her realness. They shot her compliment after compliment as well. Morgan said, "Can a bitch get a drink or something?" She said it in the voice that Method Man used in the movie *Belly*. They all fell out laughing again. Salt & Pepper cleared the lane for Darius's new catch and they both poured their attention into Jason. Darius handed Morgan a bottle of Bellaire and said, "I thought that you were with those guys over there. You don't think that they will feel a way?"

Morgan laughed, "Hell no! Prez is my big brother. If anything, he and his cronies wanted me away from them because they feel like I'm still a baby. They don't want me to see them drinking, smoking, and hearing them talk nasty to those hoes. Well, not all of them are hoes, my friend Ash is over there. She is the light one with the blond bob."

Darius couldn't believe it. Morgan, THE Morgan from the city, was all over him. She was balling with him in his booth and everyone saw it. Before today, Darius had always felt like a sheltered lame. Today he felt like the king. He looked up at Jason and he was in between a light and dark sandwich. It had all of a sudden become obvious that the two were bisexual and they were going to use Jason as a stage prop in their movie tonight. Morgan stood up to dance in Darius's face. He sipped his bottle and thought to himself, "Now this is the life." When the club was getting ready to let out, Prez walked over and told Morgan to come on. Darius was not happy at all about her leaving. To his surprise she said, "I'm cool big bruh. This is my homeboy from the city. He is going to take me to breakfast and drop me off back at my room. Prez gave Darius a look over and a nod of approval. He slapped some chick's giant ass, put his arm around her, and headed for the exit. He then turned around and said, "Oh, by the way, Ash left with one of those dudes that run with Aaron Broadnax." Jason said, "Well, I guess that's our cue," and the two drunken beauties that had him smothered for a large portion of the night grabbed each of his arms and they all walked out together. Jason turned around and yelled, "I'm riding with them I'll see you in the morning bruh." Darius gave Jason a swift nod then turned to Morgan and said, "Your chariot awaits you my queen." Morgan burst out laughing. She stood up, fixed her skirt, and grabbed Darius's hand allowing him to help her down from the booth. Morgan saw other girls from back home eyeing her and Darius. They all had the, *who the fuck is he,* face. Darius learned a valuable lesson from Jason tonight. Women may like money, jewelry, cars etc. but what truly motivates a woman when it comes to a man is the attention that he gets from other beautiful women. Darius had money that Morgan had yet to see, but it was beautiful women that broke through Morgan's wall. Those women were the direct reason that Morgan was comfortable being on his arm while leaving the club that night. As they stood at the valet stand waiting on the car to pull up. Morgan noticed the 41mm Presidential Rolex on his arm with no diamonds. Most of the women back home got excited over diamonds. They knew nothing of diamond quality nor could they distinguish between a reputable brand watch and just a shiny watch. His watch cost $35k or better and the average chick wouldn't have noticed it at all. Morgan was so glad that she grew up around her brothers and his friends. Most of the girls back home chased the appearance of what they believe to be money and would always end up wet. The men in her life taught her to recognize real money. The money that only real women and rich white folks could see. The money that isn't displayed through flossing and that you can see in a man's swag even when he wasn't wearing jewelry or driving a whip. She didn't need his money though, Prez gave her everything that she wanted. She was twenty-eight and he had already set money aside for her to start a business whenever she decided to. His thing was that he felt like most men in the city were beneath his baby sister so he taught her to pursue nothing but quality men. Morgan was peer pressured once into letting some corny dude eat her pussy and dude bragged about it to everyone. Her brother almost choked the life out of her, then made her call the guy up and offer him sex. When the guy showed up, he ran into whoever Prez sent to handle him. The only thing Morgan knew was that no one ever saw the guy again. After that, everyone that she dated had to show some sort of good quality that other men respected. Normally Prez would have grilled her about Darius. It was obvious that he seen or knew something about him because he left her in his care without saying a word. Morgan smiled on the inside when his car pulled up. It was the luxury Volkswagen that was only a few years old. It was before it's time and didn't catch on with the public, however real car enthusiast knew it was loaded like a Bentley but as low key as a Honda. The perfect whip for a guy who liked to enjoy luxury but didn't want to flex. Flashy guys made Morgan hold out. They had to really work to get her and most never succeeded. Now on the flip side, a guy like Darius was definitely a keeper. She could tell that he would cherish her and wasn't into just knocking off a bunch of women just to say that he did it. If she did give him some, he would appreciate it. The dilemma of being a polished woman and having a brother that held you accountable for your actions meant that you couldn't always get your itch scratched when you needed it. When you did find a decent guy, you sometimes came off like a whore because you threw that pussy on him faster than a Tasmanian devil. Men are idiots in that area. They tend to think that women don't just get horny and want to fuck but women have needs too, and just like men are ok with saying "Oh, I fucked her", so are women at times. She laughed at her freaky thoughts as they entered the car and wondered what type of crazy turns this night would take. One thing she knew for sure, was that she was definitely going along for the ride.

Waffle House, IHOP, and Gladys Knights were all extremely crowded. Darius said that his hotel had 24-hour room service and there was seating on the balcony in his room where they could eat. He also made it clear that this was not an attempt to get her to his room and if she wished to deal with the 1 1/2 wait at Waffle House, he was willing to do so just so she could feel comfortable. Morgan had already sized him up. He was short, solid and built like he could lift a tank, but he seemed soft. He didn't seem to have a violent bone in his body. He had a round baby face with a look in his eyes that said he was a hopeless romantic. Every time she would say something to him, he looked her in the face and opened his eyes wide to show that she had his full attention. An attentive man was a sexy man in Morgan's eyes; she honestly felt that she could fuck him up if need be, so she felt perfectly comfortable around him.

Breakfast on the balcony was amazing. You could tell that Darius and Jason didn't spare a dollar on their suite. The balcony overlooked Lenox Mall and the rest of the Buckhead area. The Atlanta streets were a lot busier than those of Cincinnati at 4am on a Sunday night. She once heard that when the President of the United States had to stay overnight in Atlanta, he stayed at this same hotel. By the looks of the room, with its purple and gold comforter that was fit for nothing less than royalty, it's granite counters, marble floors, beautiful pictures, and thick plush carpet made the room feel as if you weren't even in the United States. This had to be what a room in Paris would look like. She was now eager to get to know Darius; where did he hang? What did he do? Who did he screw? She figured Darius to be some suburban guy that had a drug connection based outside of the inner city. He probably used Jason to meet people being that Jason had a lot of inner city connections due to his barbershop down in the hood. She couldn't come right out and ask if he was a hustler though. She figured that she would just pick his drunken brain. To her surprise, Darius came from money. He had well to do parents and several college degrees. He was actually the guy that used to own the high end local clothing line *Waldorf Conceptions* back in the day. For the last 8 years he had been running a construction company that he inherited from a friend of his dad. With his sales and marketing background, he had pushed the construction company to peaks never imagined by his dad and his partners. She was correct; he was a square with money.

"What's a suburban business man like you doing with a guy that owns a barbershop in the hood?" she asked. She wanted to know exactly how Darius knew Jason.

"Jason and I were college buddies. Jason was always the people friendly guy that got me into parties and through or over a lot of the pitfalls that came with being a square from the suburbs. I know I don't smoke marijuana, but did you know that the guys in the hood charged suburb guys $200 more for an ounce of Kush than they did guys from the hood?" Morgan could believe it because her brother and his crew did a lot of business with suburban white hustlers who they said paid top dollar to get their hands on certain quality drugs.

Switching the topic, she asked, "Why aren't you married?"

"I always meet the square and boring women. On paper, they have it all together but romantically they are almost always a dud. I tried dating more "hood/street" women but even they have been complete nightmares. I have been hurt so I will admit that I am somewhat bitter. Not towards women in general, but towards the way that this capitalistic society causes people to act at times." He explained.

"I agree. On more than one occasion I have seen women try to love a man that they really didn't like simply because he had money. On the flip side, I have seen men try to make a good woman out of a bad one simply because she was attractive." She said. Morgan also wondered if real love was just a thing of the past. Could it be something that our parents and grandparents would tell us about yet we would never experience it?

Darius said, "Enough about me. Tell me about you Ms. Morgan. How much plastic surgery did it require to get a face and teeth so perfect? Most importantly, how much did that fake butt cost?" She burst out laughing and Darius did as well. "But seriously though, tell me all about yourself. I am eager to know everything about you from your childhood to now, whether it be good, bad, or embarrassing. If I am going to marry you, I have to be sure that you don't have childhood issues that have caused you to become a serial killer that chops up men." Morgan swung from across the table, punching Darius in the shoulder. "Owwww dammit! You hit hard and you have reach like a boxer."

She laughed and said, "Well, since you want to know about me, let me start by saying this: I will beat your ass negro! I have been taking Israeli martial arts since I was twelve and yoga since seven and kick as hard as I punch. No childhood trauma; I wasn't molested or anything like that and

I don't have self-esteem issues. Even though my dad was a hustler, he was always around so I don't have daddy issues either. I have plenty of female friends so I'm not clingy. Believe it or not, I went to private school. I graduated from 7 Hills and have a ton of white friends, male and female. I'm currently managing the bar that I own back home, Club Fire, as well as some rental property that I inherited from my father. My brother had the buildings fully renovated so that I wouldn't be plagued with constant repairs and all of my tenants pay on time. Owning those buildings and the club has helped me to focus on me, and trying to figure out what is that I was really put on this earth to do. Most men and women back home think that I'm a sack chaser and to be honest, they are right. The difference with me is that I want a well to do man strictly for the purpose of adding to what I am already doing, not just to have him taking care of me." Darius was awe struck. He had previously assumed that she was just a hood beauty, a very shallow one at that. This woman just debunked his theory about her. "And by the way, I've never had sex with a black guy. I've had my pussy eaten by one, but there was never any penetration. Growing up, guys from the neighborhood were afraid of me because of my brother. I was forced to do all of my naughty stuff with white guys that I went to school with. It wasn't until recently that my brother agreed to back off and respect the fact that I am old enough to make my own decisions. Normally he would have grilled you before he left me with you. Shit, he probably wouldn't have allowed me to stay, but he did. He trusted you with his prize possession, you should feel special."

Darius could have sat and talked to Morgan all night but

he looked at the clock and seen a bright red 5:30 am and said, "I see time has gotten beside us. You can stay here tonight and take Jason's bed in the adjoining suite if you would like. Housekeeping came in earlier and cleaned the rooms so the sheets are fresh.

Morgan burst out laughing, "You must didn't hear a word that I said! I have been sheltered and overprotected my entire life. I've been kept completely tucked away from black men. I'm on vacation and my brother has taken his shackles off of me. I want to jump up and down on the bed naked, play house, footsies, and keep you up all morning."

Darius laughed as well and realized how much he admired her easy going personality. She asked him for a t-shirt and some lotion and he obliged.

"Do you have a Sprite or a Ginger Ale in your hotel fridge? My stomach hurts?" Morgan said in a bitchy tone.

Darius checked the fridge, and all that he had was water. Once he got things situated for her, he left in search of a soda machine. Finding a sprite proved to be an adventure being that the entire hotel was probably hung over. He managed to buy one from the coffee shop in the hotel lobby. As he rode the elevator back up to the room, he allowed his mind to align with his penis. Morgan had a big mouth and if the opportunity presented itself, he wanted to give her something that would shut her mouth for good. When he returned to the room, he was immediately blessed with the image of Morgan lying on her back with her legs spread wide and holding both of her feet up near her head in a yoga position. He was so caught off guard that he said, "what the fuck?" He didn't even notice that he said it out loud.

She laughed and said, "I don't want the sprite, can you just kiss it and make it better?" Darius was stunned. He definitely didn't expect her to be so open and free. Most women of Morgan's caliber liked to play a lot of teasing games. Women like her wanted to put on pajamas and have a long drawn out discussion with you about how you better not be expecting to get any. Now here she was in front of him, legs spread. Even if she wasn't trying to have sex with him at the moment it was on him to try and get her to cave in. He was about to have a panic attack when she said, " don't try to kiss my goods either you creep... I want you to kiss my tummy, rub it, and make it feel better."

Darius let out a huge sigh of relief because he wasn't well versed in giving oral pleasure to women and he didn't want to disappoint her, but the way that she was laying there made her look edible to say the least. As he eased onto the bed to kiss her stomach, he couldn't help but to look at her pretty, pink, wet vagina... It was calling him. He gently kissed her starting right below her breast and moved down to her navel. He felt his nature rise as she began to squirm. He kissed below her navel and she pulled back further on her legs causing her vagina to protrude. Darius took that as an open invite and kissed it. He gave her pretty pink slit a long slow lick from bottom to top. The relaxing sound that she made lit Darius's fire. He was so hard that it hurt, and he yearned for her to feel him. He prayed that she wasn't one of those women that got a man all the way there and then said, "I can't do this." She was juicy and he wanted her juices all over his face. He closed his mouth and tried to put his entire face into her wetness. He figured that if she concluded that he was a nasty freak, she wouldn't hesitate to sample what else he could do. He stuck his tongue out while inside of her and attempted to lick the inner workings of her love hole, causing her to say his name under her breath. Morgan was moaning in such an appreciative manner that he figured he was doing it right even though he lacked experience. Now it was time to really freak her. He kissed his way back up her sexy chocolate torso; making sure that he kissed, licked, and nibbled every inch of her body in route to her succulent lips. Licking and kissing on her neck while using his finger to pleasure her clitoris caused Morgan to arch her back. To his surprise, she grabbed hold of his face and began kissing him passionately. She hadn't lied to him, just by the way that she moaned, he could tell that she was a woman who needed to be touched. The sound of her splashy wetness and the stickiness of his fingers had Darius on the verge of a climax. He eased his way down, sucking and licking on her clitoris in the most aggressive manner imaginable. Morgan forced her legs down and started kicking in an attempt to run from his tongue. He licked and sucked as if his life depended on it. She tried to pull away as her right leg began to shake, but Darius held her down by the hips. She must have had an orgasm because she jerked violently, and screamed his name, "Dariussssss!"

Morgan hopped up and started kissing Darius's face, eager to reciprocate. She wanted all of her juices back and she plunged her tongue deep into his mouth as if she was trying to retrieve them. It just felt so right giving herself to Darius. It seemed as if he had been her lover for years. He needed to be pleased. She could tell by his demeanor that he had only had sex before and had never experienced a woman hell bent on pleasing him. She sat him down on the edge of the bed, pulling his pants off. She got down on her knees like a two-dollar whore and took Darius into her mouth. She gulped down every inch of him while massaging his strong inner thighs like the white girls at her private school taught her. The way that he was twisting and trying to run made her doubt if Darius had ever known such pleasure. She slowly eased him up out of her throat and proceeded to lick every inch of his manhood. While massaging his testicles she took a long slow lick up his shaft. She felt him jerk, so she used her hand to pull all of his cum up out of him. Every muscle in his short, massive frame tensed and flexed. She thought, had he been her man, maybe she would have swallowed it for the first time. Darius wasn't done though. Thoughts of her with her legs back were still stuck in his mind. He pushed her back on the bed and entered her. Her vagina was virgin tight. She squirmed like she was trying to get away, but he eased everything he had into her. She had been talking shit since the day he encountered her at the wing spot, now she was here, stuck up under his manhood. He compensated for what god didn't give him in height in the length of his penis. She was about to get this best pounding of her life. Morgan didn't know what to do with herself. This little short fucker was huge; she felt as if a baseball bat was inside of her. None of the white boys that she had been with scratched the surface of how deep he was. He wasn't letting her move, so all that she could do was brace herself for the pounding. Darius gave her slow and calculated strokes while sucking on her ample breast. He really enjoyed how she was squirming in an attempt to get away, it brought out the animal in him. He finally felt that extra splash of wetness come, signaling that her vagina was all the way ready for him. He pushed her legs back and began to dig deep into her stomach. He made sure that with every stroke he pulled 11 of his 12 inches up out of her, and shoved 11 back in.

"You have been talking crazy to me since the first time we came into contact! I got you now, and you are about to pay for every word, and every insult that you have sent my way." Darius said while shoving his dick deep into her.

"Aaaaahhhhhhh!" Morgan screamed. She felt as though he was trying to kill her!

"Don't 'ahhhhh' now," Darius said while taking a push up sort of stance over Morgan. "Say you are sorry, say you are sorry!!!" He had her going wild! Her vagina was soaking wet and the more he pounded, the more he knew that he had just seduced his soul mate.

"Darius! I'm sorry, oh my god daddy I'm so sorry baby ahhhhhhhh!" Morgan screamed.

Morgan had never felt such painful pleasure. This little bitty man was taking her to new orgasmic heights. He was so strong, long, big, aggressive and controlling, and she loved it. She loved him! *"Oh shit!"* she thought to herself. He had just made her say that she loved him. Just then Morgan felt the thrust that broke the camel's back. She was his, he had taken her soul away from her. Darius pulled out of Morgan just as she seemed to pass out. He let his wad explode all over her pretty, flat stomach. He had left his mark, Morgan now knew who the man was.

The next morning, while Darius was still asleep,

Morgan snuck out on the balcony to make a phone call. Her pussy lips were inflamed and throbbing as if they had a heartbeat, not to mention she felt like her insides were gone.

"Ash are you up?" Morgan asked.

"Yes, where are you? You didn't come to the room last night?" Ash replied in a frustrated and sleepy voice.

"I'm still with the guy Darius that I left the club with. Did you get on?" Morgan asked.

"Hell no, he is right here. He was so drunk that he passed out." Ash said.

Morgan laughed, "Well don't worry girlfriend because I took enough dick for the both of us last night!"

"Biiiiiitcccchhhh!!!!!" Ash screamed as she slammed the phone down.

CHAPTER EIGHT

"TWO WORLDS COLLIDE"

Ameesha walked back to her office thinking about what her friend Jeanean said about her date the previous night. Was it really that bad out here? Had they just gotten too old to get the respect, time and effort of today's men? Had her and her group of friends become unattractive? Was opening doors, covering a woman's hair after she had it done just for you, giving her your undivided attention on a date etc., become extinct? Things that used to be normal in the past seemed to be rocket science today. She knew one thing though, she may have yet to find the man of her dreams in the circles of people that she ran in, but she damn sure wasn't going to stoop to dealing with hustlers and street dudes as some of her female peers and colleagues had. She wasn't trying to get shot, or worse, end up dead for being around the wrong guy. Especially after what had happened to Lonzo...

***

It had been 8 years since Lonzo was murdered and since she had seriously dated anyone. From time to time, when she couldn't bare plastic loving anymore, she would choose a cute co-worker or suitor to fuck the shit out of for a few weeks. None of them were ever worth keeping because they didn't match the drive and promise that she seen in Lonzo. It wasn't a money thing either, but she wanted a man with a big plan, big dreams, or one that she could impregnate with "Lonzo's Plan". She still dreamed of his business utopia idea for blacks in Cincinnati and her dying wish was to see that plan come to fruition.

The honk of the horn from a passing car snapped her back to reality. She figured that if it was hard enough to get men of the corporate world to act right half the time, then what could a woman possibly expect from a thug? Well, at least it was payday, and she and the girls were hanging out tonight. After work she planned to go to the bank, drop her son off to her mom, and grab a couple of bottles of Merlot. She would have a couple of pregame glasses of wine before heading down to happy hour at Club 321.

Cantrell had just sold his grandmothers car to an elderly couple that paid him in cash. He figured that he would deposit the money into her account for her. Too many people came through her house and he would hate to see her money come up missing. As Cantrell exited his car in the bank's parking lot, he spotted the most beautiful and seemingly polished woman that he had ever seen. She took off walking fast before he could get a better look.

Ameesha eyed some thug looking guy getting out of a car across from hers. She prayed that this wouldn't be the day that she gets robbed or shot by some fool who was trying to steal her purse. He looked as if he was hurrying behind her and she was scared to death. The door to the damn bank seemed a mile away.

By the way the woman was walking, Cantrell thought to himself that she must have had to use the restroom or something. He was trying to get a peek at her before she entered the bank, but she was rushing to the door so fast that he knew it wasn't going to happen.

Ameesha was sure that she was going to be robbed, but at least there was nothing in her purse. The mugger was going to get to her before she got to the door. She wanted to scream for help but was too afraid to even get a word out.

Cantrell made it to the door just in time to hold it for the woman. He opened it and said, "Ladies first."

Ameesha felt her heart rise again. It had initially dropped to her stomach, and she had been terrified. She couldn't believe that this big guy in a black hoodie had just rushed to open the door for her. Once inside the bank, she noticed that he was trying to watch her without watching her. He snuck several peeks while filling out his deposit slip. They were at teller's right next to one another, and she noticed that he had tossed a huge wad of cash up on the counter. She figured that he must be a drug dealer because they were the only ones who weren't afraid to walk around with wads of cash like that. She had to admit it though, Mr. Robbery Guy was a cutie. A little too edgy for her taste, but cute nonetheless. As Ameesha exited the bank, Mr. Robbery Guy exited too. She was no longer afraid of him. She whipped out her phone to call Jeanean to see what time they were going to 321. Jeanean didn't answer so she left a message, "Nean, give me a call… trying to see what time we are heading down to happy hour."

CHAPTER NINE

"THE CHASE"

Cantrell had previously heard about Club 321, and he knew if he wanted to see that woman again, he would have to go there tonight. He definitely wanted her, but he heard that it was just a club full of office people and he would feel like a fish out of water amongst that crowd. He hated being in clubs around guys that tried to dance but couldn't. It had been a long time since a woman captured his eye. The last woman that had his attention was Kia. He had some of the best times of his life with her; she was smart, cute, funny, and had a beautiful spirit. Kia was what folks would call a "square" chick though. She was clueless to everything about him and his world, and at times, this made her hard to relate to or talk to. He and Kia were lovers and friends. She would stay at his place for weeks on occasion, and sometimes he'd stayed at hers. They just loved to just be around one another. On some days, he would be sitting on the couch reading a book and she would be sitting in the chair reading a magazine. For hours they wouldn't say a word to one another;

just every once in a while one of them would look up because they would feel the other one staring and smile. That was a beautiful time in Cantrell's life. He figured if he could get his act together, he would ask Kia to marry him. She had a great job at the bank and he had his own thing going, but he couldn't keep his penis out of other women. One day her curiosity got the best of her. She went through his phone, seen all of the text, pics, and emails from other women, and flipped out. Eventually her insecurities in relation to him got the best of her and they were forced to call it quits.

Thanks to Maarku, when Cantrell got out of the prison, he had developed a disdain for senseless material goods. Maarku helped him understand the wealth that lies within family, love, happiness, knowledge, and understanding. By the graces of Allah, Cantrell now stood on the outside looking in. He saw all of the foolery in his own actions and clearly understood that it takes a good woman to free a man from the *trap*. That was the reason he was going to find this woman. There was just something that he sensed about her while inside the bank; she seemed like she could be a breath of fresh air. Cantrell pulled out his phone, and logged into Facebook using his cousin's info. He wanted to view pics from the Happy Hour on DJ Paul's page. As he scrolled through the pics, he didn't see anyone that he knew personally and the majority of the people seemed to be from a totally different planet than him. It didn't matter to him though, being his mom's only child Cantrell was used to being alone. In all actuality, he loved being alone and keeping to himself; it gave him a sense of peace.   He always went places on his own, rather it be to a restaurant to eat or to a bar to watch the game. He was determined to go to the club to find this woman if it was the last thing that he did.

He searched through various albums of the club pictures looking for someone that could give him an idea of what he needed to wear to fit in at the club. There was an assortment of guys dressed in horrible suits that weren't tailored; there were guys rocking the sweater tied around the neck and one around the waist look, but that look wasn't for him. He eyed a guy whose name was tagged as Christian Bradford in a photo. He seemed to have an unorthodox sense of style; nothing matched, but everything worked. He had on tan fitted dress slacks with a blue blazer that resembled the ones that the kids wore in Catholic schools. Underneath, he rocked a loud colored checkered shirt, with a bow tie that made it all look fresh. Dude was definitely office fly. Cantrell had a few nice blazers and slacks at home in his closet that he had purchased for when he attended office parties with Kia. As far as shirts and ties went, his uncle Roscoe had him covered. He may have been a grease monkey, but he had boxes of tailored shirts, and an assortment of ties, belts, handkerchiefs etc. that Cantrell could wear. He just refused to rock Unc's suits because they were too old school. It was almost eerie how much Cantrell had grown to resemble his uncle. They were the exact same size, and from the pics in his mom's photo album, he looked just like his uncle did at his age.

When Cantrell pulled into his garage, he began to ponder what he would do if he did get Ms. Thang's attention. She seemed to be one of those scary and nerdy type of women who tended to shun guys like him. He had several encounters in the past where he was introduced to a female friend of a woman that one of his friends were dating. He recalled the worst time of his life in detail: he was called to go out to eat with Michael (his real estate agent), his girlfriend, and her friend. As soon as they sat down at the dinner table, the friend who introduced herself to him as Tanya began to talk nonstop about her degrees and job title. She left no room for him to say a single word, yet the next day she told Michael's girlfriend that he wasn't like Michael. She complained about how he couldn't hold an intelligent conversation without even realizing that she talked nonstop for 2 hours about herself, leaving no room for him to insert himself into the conversation and make his impression.

As he entered his place through the garage, he envisioned how Ms. Thang would take to his place, if he managed to get her. He had inherited a car shop with a small warehouse attached to it from his uncle Roscoe that sat on a side street off on Central Parkway up near Cincinnati State. He remodeled it to look like one of those fancy lofts downtown. It took him two years to get it done, even while using the Mexican construction crew that one of his connections had introduced him to. It wasn't the ideal area, but by leaving the outside of the place as is, it still gave off the old car repair shop appearance. When the garage doors opened while entering the building, or if you happened to glance in from the street, you would see tools and hoses hanging from the ceiling. A person would never dream of what lied behind those doors. Once you entered the key code, it opened to a 3000 sq. ft. loft; complete with spiral staircases, sky lights, a functioning cargo elevator that went from the living room to the master bedroom, a master bath complete with a stand-alone shower, Jacuzzi tub, double sink counter, a huge master closet, and a separate room with a 10 person Jacuzzi. There was Bluetooth surround sound throughout the entire house, and the house itself was completely sound proof. The decor of the place looked like something straight out of a magazine. He had given a local decorator whom he was dating at the time a 30 grand budget to lay out the loft, and to say that she laid it out would be an understatement. He had the finest contemporary living room and bedroom furniture straight out of Bova. His king sized bed was a pillow top that made him feel as if he was sleeping on the clouds at night. His daughter's room was laid out as well. It was pink and chrome themed with a twin bed giving her room a more modern appearance verses the medieval theme that she used throughout the rest of the house. The decorations and curtains were a mixture of expensive and affordable items that worked very well together. His full service kitchen equipped with stainless steel everything looked as if it should be in a mansion in Indian Hills. Some would say that he was a fool for putting so much money into a property that wasn't in a good area but to him it made perfect sense. It was away from the hood, and even if someone saw him coming or going from the building, it wouldn't ring an alarm because of the outward appearance of the property. The home was complete with impenetrable doors, a super alarm system, security cameras, and two pit bulls that freely roamed the garage space, so intrusion was virtually impossible.

He turned on his thinking music, Beethoven's greatest hits, and stripped down to his boxers going straight to his pull-up rack. He looked at the clock and determined that he had one hour before he needed to leave out of the house. He wanted to get downtown, grab some sushi, and then hit the club once the crowd started to form. As he busted out set after set of pull ups and dips, he reflected back on his life and all of the drama and violence that he had been raised in or around. He fought so hard to find a sense of peace within himself as well as with life. It was time for him to have a life, a woman, and maybe even another child. He was even willing to move from his place into the house with the white picket fence if need be, he just needed more from life than what he was getting.

The music and his thoughts carried Cantrell through 10 sets of 10 on the pull-up bar and 10 sets of 10 dips. He turned towards his full body length mirror to admire his hard work. At age 35, he still had his youthful athletic figure, and if anything he had added more muscle to an already nice frame. He stared with admiration at his perfect flesh; he had a few scars, but no tats. He didn't have anything against tattoos, but he never had any images that he wanted permanently on his body. He walked up the stairs to his bedroom and entered the master bath. He pressed the 'relaxation' button on his electronic shower. Removing his boxers, he stepped in and allowed the hot water and rhythm to do its job.

Freshly showered, he threw on a pair of his Alfani boxers, as well as an Alfani t-shirt. He preferred those because they were thinner and softer than the other brands. He sprayed on his favorite cologne, Creed, and headed downstairs to get dressed. He opted for a gray blazer and dark blue slacks. He chose a white shirt, and a yellow, blue, and red checkered tie that he had found in one of his uncle's old boxes. As he glanced in the mirror at himself, he thought about when was the last time that he wanted to actually pursue a woman? Nowadays women were the aggressors. He always found himself on a date or in bed with women that somehow knew him, even though he had no clue as to who they were prior to them pushing down on him. Those women didn't spark his interest when it came down to dating and courting, but this woman was pulling everything up out of him. He was already going through great lengths and venturing out of his comfort zone just to have a chance to see her again, he couldn't even imagine what he would be willing to do to have her.

Cantrell didn't know exactly what it was that he would do to get her attention, yet he was confident that he was man enough to do whatever it took. After straightening his tie, he thought to himself, "How could she deny a brother this fly?" He ran back upstairs to grab his Nixon watch out of its case. It was clean a clean and classy watch that was for occasions like these where flashy could be viewed as a turn off. He had other watches, iced out watches at that, but he didn't feel that he needed to impress this woman in that type of way. Tonight would be all about being a perfect gentleman and displaying his old school courting abilities. All these politics nowadays about should men have to pay for a woman's drinks? Who should pay on the first date? That was the least of his worries. He knew how to get Ms. Thang, he just needed her to get where he could see her.

CHAPTER TEN

"HAPPY HOUR"

As Cantrell drove down to the club, he concocted his plan; he wouldn't just walk up to the young lady if she did show up with her girls. He would sit back and observe what types of guys she talked to, what types of female friends she hung out with, how was she dressed, what she drank etc. He felt like a million bucks with his suit tailored to fit like a glove. His friends would say that he looked gay in such a fitted outfit; in the hood, loose seemed to be symbolic of gangster. "To hell with them dumb ass negroes," he said while laughing to himself. He couldn't get caught in a club pic at 321 though. If his homies caught whiff of this, he would definitely get clowned. They would be calling him Maxwell or John Legend for the rest of the year, the thought made him laugh. He opted to forgo the sushi, if it caused his stomach to hurt it could ruin his night, so he just ate a couple of fruit and nut bars to hold him off.

Cantrell made it to the club in less than 10 minutes, the time was 6 pm sharp. He knew that he had to see this woman again, yet he didn't want her to notice him before he had a chance to make his observations. How could he blend in when all of the dudes that frequented the spot either went to school together or knew one another from work? He heard that it was like a fraternity in that place, the people only dealt with or talked to the people in their respective circles. All of this was going through his mind as he parked his truck valet and walked towards the club's entrance.

He had never been to a club that had white bouncers before. All of the clubs that he'd been to, he always knew the bouncers from somewhere. He never got patted down at his spots, but the big buffed white bouncers at the door of 321 reminded him of the ones in the intake part of the Detention Center. As he showed his ID, they started to pat him down. They wanted to go all in his pants, around the back of his waistline, and lifted up his pants legs. He felt like he had just been raped by the bouncers, he hoped that Ms. Thang was worth the hassle. Thank God he had on some fly socks and underwear because they completely exposed his under garments during the search. The ladies in line behind him would have laughed at him if they weren't some fly shit.

The club had a decent crowd. It wasn't shoulder to shoulder crowded but it had a strong and flowing happy hour crowd. All of his perceived notions were confirmed; he saw the office buddies, the frat brothers, the law enforcement and fire fighter guys, the corny dancing dudes, as well as the ever present Walnut Hills alumni guys and all of them were in their respective crowds. Even with the music blasting, he heard a voice coming from the dance floor area, it was a voice that he had been hearing since the 4th grade, Darwin

Carmichael's. He had been dancing since they were kids and he was currently tearing up the dance floor, and showing the corny dancers how to bust a move. Cantrell decided not to speak to Darwin because he could be long winded and he had no time to waste catching up on old times. He was on a mission to capture the lady that caught his eye earlier at the bank. He wasn't really a drinker, but he grabbed a glass of merlot to sip as he made his way to a corner. Even being ducked off, he felt eyes on him from every angle. He knew that he didn't fit in; the guys were looking at him and he could see them whispering to one another, "Who is he?" A few chicks looked his way, and one heavyset but very cute woman walked over and offered to buy him a drink. He politely declined the drink but he jokingly commented about her protruding breast. He asked could he put one of those things in a head lock and she laughed. He informed her that he was waiting on someone. She respected that, yet she still shot him a flirtatious look as she walked away. Cantrell was growing impatient because clubs weren't his thing. He never fared well around a bunch of people that he didn't know. He checked his watch and it was 6:30pm. He had only been there for 30 minutes, yet it seemed like a life time. There were still no signs of Ms. Thang, but he was determined to wait until at least 8:30 to see if she would come. The odd stares from the men and seductive stares from the more aggressive women were zoning him out. There was a chick standing at the bar with her girls a few feet from him. She stood out because she had a loud and goofy voice, but a body like Serena Williams. This chick was thick in all of the right places and small in all of the right places, but she did that irritating snorting thing when she laughed. She had on some simple gray work slacks and a white blouse, but the slacks hugged her hips and butt so perfectly that you would have thought she had on tights. It was almost a crime to be that sexy but goofy at the same time. Darwin once told him at a Final Friday that chicks like that have the best pussy in the world and are the biggest freaks.

He tried to stay focused on the matter at hand, but if Ms. Thang didn't get there soon, he was definitely going to push up on Ms. Goofy. Thirty more minutes passed and Cantrell was starting to grow impatient. He figured that bumping into Ms. Thang must not have been meant to be. He opted to send a round or two to Ms. Goofy and her girls, to see if maybe he could slide in Ms. Goofy tonight. She seemed like the easy type that wouldn't recognize real game when it hit her. As he walked towards the bar he couldn't help but slump, this was the first time in a very long time that he had felt this way about a woman. He had his heart set on seeing her, and hopefully making some sort of connection with her tonight. He ordered himself a double shot of Patron to ease the pain, then sent an anonymous round to Ms. Goofy and her friends. He walked back to his spot in the corner, listening as Ms. Goofy and crew got over excited about receiving a free round. Just as he leaned his back up against the wall in defeat, she walked in.

Ms. Thang and her friends walked over to the bar next to Ms. Goofy and her crew, immediately causing them to frown their faces. Ms. Thang didn't roll with slouches either, the chick to her right was brown skinned, short, but built like a gymnast. The chick on her left was model height, red bone, and cute with a body that seemed to have been preserved well over her years. Her only flaw was that she over did it on the make up in his opinion. He glanced back at Ms. Thang in awe. "Oh my God," he thought to himself. She looked ten times better than she did earlier at the bank. She was beyond fine, beyond attractive, and beyond stunning, she was just plain jaw dropping beautiful. She had on a simple but fitted red dress. It was sleek with a slight plunged neck line that allowed a peek-a-boo view of her cleavage. Her heels weren't the extremely tall ones that women wore to accentuate their butt; they were the short and comfortable office type of heels, yet her butt still looked robust. The shoes and the dress made her look like a sexy librarian. Her hair was pulled straight back into a pony tail revealing nothing but natural beauty and angelic facial features, very light make up if any over seemingly flawless skin, and clear lip gloss. Nowadays it's rare to see a woman confident enough to step out without a long weave hanging down her back, and an overly beat face. She had that simple but banging beauty thing going on and he was all wrapped up in it. Her hips were the set off, women were paying for hips and ass like she had. She wasn't extremely thick but you could tell that as she aged, she would only fill out even more in a good way. Her calves looked as those of a woman who ran track, and he hoped that those calves were connected to feet that had pretty toes. He found a corner with a better viewing angle, and posted up like a lion waiting to pounce on prey. Ms. Thang seemed to be known amongst this circle of women, but not necessarily very popular. Every woman that she walked by or bumped into waved as if they knew her and her friends, but they didn't try to hold a conversation with them. The men acted the opposite; they threw themselves at her. Cantrell had to laugh

104

because it was obvious that none of those dudes had any game. After making her rounds, her and her girls sat at a small VIP section that was very close to where he was standing. He could somewhat hear their conversation amidst the music. He overheard her telling them about how she almost passed out running from a thug in the bank's parking lot, and how he ended up being a perfect gentleman, a very handsome one at that. That last comment made Cantrell chuckle. He wondered if she had paid him any attention earlier, and she had just answered his question. He figured if he caught her eye in a hoodie, she would be elated to see him all decked out; especially once he explained that he came down to try and catch her, and only her. He spied a guy walking towards her VIP section. He was one of those guys that rocked too many clothes at once; a hat, a polo, a sweater over the polo, a sweater around the neck, and a scarf, he was definitely the clown type. He must have asked Ms. Thang if he could but her a drink. Cantrell heard that and thought to himself that the guy had no class. It's common practice amongst real gentlemen to offer the woman that he is pursuing a drink but he has to say, "Can I buy you and your friends and drink?" Needless to say, she turned her nose up at the idiot, appalled at the way he ignored her girls as if they were not sitting there too. Cantrell saw dudes flaw as his opportunity. He slid away to the bar and asked the bartender to personally deliver a bottle of Moët to the ladies table, and to specifically tell Ms. Thang that it was for her and her friends. He hurried back to his spot, not wanting to draw the attention of the ladies, as he watched the bartender approach their table with the bottle all decked out with sparklers and carrying fancy champagne flutes. The ladies were shocked.

You could tell they weren't familiar with that type of treatment amongst this particular crowd. They scanned the room for who may have sent it, initially laying their eyes on the clown with no game, but it was obvious that he never went to the bar. After a few minutes, they seemed to have given up on trying to figure out who sent it. They started to drink up, dance, and shake off the edge of an obviously long work week as most folks do at Happy Hours. Ms. Thang got up and walked towards the restroom, he saw her stagger just a bit, laughed. One thing was for certain though, she had a real grown woman sexy but classy swagger about her. Cantrell never took his eyes off of the ladies' room. Each direct glimpse of her made him feel a step closer to connecting with her. He watched as she emerged, making it past all of the thirsty fellas and hating women. He put his head down as she walked back towards their table, and his direction. He didn't want to get caught staring. He was responding to a text in his phone, when he saw a pair of women's shoes almost stepping on his feet. He looked up and saw that it was her, Ms. Thang. She said, "Thank you for the bottle Mr. Stalker." He was lost for words. He thought to himself, "How in the hell did she know that it was me?" She must have read his mind because she continued, "I come here too often. I've known this same crowd of people minus a few for over 12 years and as a woman, we scour the room for new faces male and female. You sir, stuck out like a sore thumb. It didn't take us long to figure that you were the one who sent the bottle because you were the only guy in here that wasn't running up in these thirsty ass chicks faces." He was too embarrassed to laugh. She spoke so direct that it made him shrink up and act shy. He tried to talk but all that he could do was stutter. "Where do I know you from?" she asked. He tried to explain that he just thought that she was attractive so he sent her a bottle, but she caught him in his lie. "You are the guy from the bank earlier! That's where I know you from! What made you come down here because I've never saw you here before?" she continued. Before he could respond, the clown from earlier walked up behind her and pulled her wrist asking could he talk to her for a second. Cantrell remained calm being that he didn't know their prior dealings or if they did have any. She responded swiftly and bluntly to the guy, "No, and I would greatly appreciate it if you would let go of my wrist sir." The guy still hadn't let go, so Cantrell grabbed the guys arm and separated it from hers in the most respectful way that he could muster. The guy got irate and went on a rant about him touching his hand. Cantrell scooped Ms. Thang up behind him with his left arm, and then stepped to the guys face. A war of words broke out between the two men and it caused the fraternity guys to run over to the guy's aid. A short shoving match ensued, but he never allowed Ms. Thang to go unprotected. He felt that she was a scrappy one because she was doing her best to get loose and help him, but he just held her back with a firm grip. The bouncers walked over and immediately sided with the regulars and started to rough Cantrell up, but he fought back. He even felt the clown sneak in a few punches. Being a man from the streets, he wasn't used to this sort of blatant disrespect, and with the influence of the alcohol, he went into a blood rage. He calmed down enough to allow himself to be thrown out as if he was some bitch ass nigga. Once he could get to his truck and grab his gun, he would come back and let loose and it would be a wrap. These cats had no clue who they were fucking with.

As he hurried to his car, he heard a scream from behind him, it was Ms. Thang. He kept walking because he was past trying to get on with her, he wanted and needed to kill somebody. He heard her scream again, she was yelling, "Your keys, you dropped your keys!" He patted his pockets, realizing that she was right, he was forced to allow her to catch up to him. She handed him his keys but immediately went into the typical female rant about how they aren't worth it, please don't do it, just leave spiel. Cantrell looked her directly in the eyes and said, "One of them niggas is dead." She screamed, "Nooooooo!!!!! I don't want to see anyone harmed or incarcerated over me, please don't do this, I won't be able to bear it! Let's just go to breakfast, give me your keys and we will ride around to Joe's, it will give you a chance to calm down." Cantrell stood firm, "Babe, I came down here tonight because I overheard you saying that you would be here. My sole purpose was to come here and attempt to connect with you, but now I've been disrespected, I just can't let that ride."

"You are drunk," she replied, "you will probably get pulled over with the gun leaving here, let me drive you home. As scared as I am to leave the club with a man that I don't know, I am willing to take a leap of faith to save you from jail as well as save a life." Trell's eyes lit up and he said, "I'm not hungry, but you can take me home."

She agreed to drive the drunk, mad man home. She figured that she would get to his place and then call her a ride from his car. Her girls were texting her wondering where she went. She let them know to turn on their family tracker to monitor where she was going and where she stopped at. They agreed to do so, so she at least felt a little comfort knowing that if this guy did kill her he would be caught. But for some reason, she felt completely safe in his presence. Maybe it was the way that he protected her in the club, or the way he opened the door for her at the bank when she thought that he was a mugger, or maybe it was the way that he looked at her in such an innocent and loving manner when he explained that he had only come down to 321 to try and meet her. She put her fears aside and prayed that the good lord would protect her. "What is your name?" she asked.

He replied, "Cantrell Solomon."

"My name is Ameesha Jones, sir and I'm so sorry that we had to meet in this manner."

He said, "I know you may feel uncomfortable being in the car with a total stranger. Feel free to look me up on the Clerk of Courts website, besides, isn't that what y'all females do? I promise you won't find any rapes or murders on my record." He looked at her and they both smiled. He was open and honest about his criminal past, while explaining his rough upbringing in an environment full of drugs and violence. He spoke so eloquently that she felt bad for him not scared, if anything he seemed to be weak and vulnerable. He was starting to dose off, so she asked for his address so she could GPS it. As Cantrell laid his head back, he played drunk and sleep. He couldn't believe that Ameesha was in his truck. He actually decided to thank the clown for the commotion because had the fight not broken out, he would have needed nothing less than a miracle to get a woman like her into his car tonight. He knew that she was afraid, and he knew that she would probably have a ride waiting for her at his place but he still felt that God himself was on his side tonight so he just might get to have a few hours in her presence if she would just spend the night. He didn't feel the need to have sex with her, he just wanted her there.

"He looks like a baby sleeping," Ameesha thought to herself, and the man smelled like heaven. When she first saw him in the club, she thought that he looked like a man out of a magazine; fit and handsome, but with a little extra edge. He was doing his best to be discreet, but a man this fine sticks out, especially in a room full of regulars. Ameesha always feared the rugged street guy types and knowing that he was from the streets definitely was a call for concern. From the look in his eyes back on the street, she could definitely tell that he was going to kill someone back at 321, but those same eyes revealed to her that he was a protector as well, one that would protect his woman and family, by any means necessary.

They arrived at the address on the GPS, and Ameesha instantly became afraid. It was an abandoned garage. He had dozed off but the car coming to a complete stop woke him up. As he sat up, he instantly realized how afraid she must be pulling up to his building. He looked over at her and saw that she was trying to hide her fears, but he understood her completely. Strange man, abandoned garage, he has a gun on him, no one around to help her, she had to be scared to death. He broke the awkward silence and asked, "Have you ever shot a gun before?"

She looked at him and said, "Me and my girls go to the shooting range at least twice a month. Why would you ask me that?"

"Reach up under your seat and grab my gun." He

encouraged her to take it off of safety, and she did as he asked. "Now I'm going to reach into my glove box to get a pen and a piece of paper. This is my number. Take my car, drive yourself home, and call me whenever you get up in the morning. You can either meet me with the car, or leave it somewhere safe and put the key under the mat, tell me where you left it, and I will get it that way. I'm not a weirdo, I have no intention on harming you so I'm going to get out now and go into my place. I know my place looks weird, but it's actually a nice place. It's not some creepy garage that I have brought you to so that I could kill you and dismember your body." He laughed, she laughed, and he exited the car. He took a few steps, and then turned back and said, "With all of the commotion tonight, I remember you saying your name, but I didn't catch it."

She said, "It's Ameesha Jones, but my close friends call me Meesh."

"Ok Ameesha. Well once again, my name is Cantrell, and my close friends call me Trell. Have a safe drive home, and a good night. Text me to let me know that you made it home safe, this Patron and wine mixed has my head spinning a little.

Ameesha watched as he hit a code on the keypad and entered the garage. As the garage door closed, she could see him going through another door that seemed to have a key pad on it as well. She was completely open to this man and still couldn't quite understand why. In the bar he carried himself as a gentleman, even while intoxicated. When he exited the truck, he didn't even ask for a hug. She decided to stop at White Castles. She didn't want the food, she just needed to park and think for a second about everything that had just occurred. This man from the bank had overheard her conversation about going to 321. He took the time out to get dressed up and come down there looking for her. He found her, circumstances led to her having to leave the club with him, yet he did nothing to try and lure her into his home. Most men would have taken that as an opportunity to try to put the moves on a woman, especially while they both were drunk. She just sat there for a while; for one she needed to sober up a bit, but for two, she secretly hoped that he would text her phone and say something like, "I wish you could have stayed". That text never came though, and she honestly had become pressed to see more of him tonight. Then a light bulb went off in her head, she figured she could call him and say that she was too drunk to drive, and that she only made it around the corner to White Castles. Maybe he could come and get her in another vehicle? Or maybe he could walk around there? Hell, she didn't care what he did, but this man needed to do something. She called his phone, he answered and said, "You made it home pretty fast; you must live close by." Ameesha replied, "I only made it to White Castles. I'm too drunk to drive for real, and somehow I must have dropped my keys in the club. I've been sitting here calling my girls, but they must have gone out to Rhinos. Ummm, my mom has my extra key, but she is sleep. This has to be the worst night ever."

Cantrell said, "I'm not sober enough to drive far, but I can walk around there to drive you and the car back here. You can sit in my place until someone answers for you."

She took a long pause and replied, "I think that would be

my best option. I'm so sorry for the inconvenience, I hope that I'm not imposing on whoever you would have been spending your Friday night with?"

He laughed and said, "Woman, having you stranded at my house fully clothed is still the best Friday night ever."

It wasn't more than ten minutes when he came walking around the corner. He had on a fitted t-shirt revealing nothing but defined muscles, with some pajama pants. It was this moment as he was approaching the truck that changed everything for Ameesha, she got a glimpse of his print. She saw it, hanging there in all of its glory! She hated life, if she had known this man for a few weeks at least, she would have his thing so far down her throat that he wouldn't be able to do anything but squeal and moan like a crying puppy. She honestly thought about being a whore for the night and just handing her goods over to him on a silver platter, but that was not an option. She had morals, standards, as well as a reputation to protect. Yet, she had walked a straight line her entire life; church, school, career, no drugs; she just felt entitled to indulge in something out of her norm. He came to the driver's side and told her to hop over as he climbed in. He still smelled like heaven, but now he smelled like a scented soap, not a cologne. Her mind wandered, she wondered did he or would he taste like fruit? And if he did, would he let her taste it without judging her? She fought with the idea of how he would take to her if she gave in to her womanly desires tonight, on the first night, shit this wasn't even the first date!

As they entered the house it smelled of burning incense. He needed to grab a few things out of the truck, so he told her to punch 1774 into the keypad so that she could go on in.

She couldn't believe that he would just trust a total stranger with his code, but for some strange reason, she would have trusted this man with her security code as well. She walked in and was stunned by the most beautiful loft that she had ever seen. The loft fit Cantrell's personality; rough outer shell, but soft insides. This guy had classical decor, beautiful granite countertops, and skylights that looked as if you could touch the stars. There was a wall full of books like the big library, complete with the rolling ladder thing to get to the books on the higher shelves. There was a giant harp in the middle of his living room. By the looks of the living room and kitchen, she could already tell that she would fall in love with the bedroom.

"Would you like some tea, water, juice, or maybe another drink?" he asked with a cute but sinister smile on his face.

She caught the joke, laughed as well and said, "Just a glass of water sir. I'm done with the liquor for a while."

He handed her the glass of water and she sat down on a bar stool at his kitchen island. He seemed hell bent on not looking at her or even really engaging her. His every word and action was from a distance. He asked had anyone answered the phone for her yet as if he was ready for her to get out. She was just about to say yes and leave when he said, "I know you are tipsy just like I am. If need be you can have my bed. I will sleep in my daughter's room, but at some point I need to lie down. I normally don't drink so my head is spinning, I should have been in bed an hour ago." She was ready to lie down as well, she looked at the clock, and it was only 11:45pm, but so much had occurred that it felt as if was 4am. She accepted the offer and he motioned her up to his bedroom.

Just like she thought, the bedroom was immaculate; complete with a 70-inch flat screen television, a big, classic wooden bedroom set, full body mirrors, and immaculate tile work in the master bath. This place of his was jaw dropping and under normally circumstances it could be panty dropping! Nothing looked extremely expensive, from the decorations to the furniture, but the actual craftsmanship that had been put into the house was amazing, and obviously well thought out. Cantrell went over to his dresser and handed her a long t-shirt and some socks. He went into the bathroom and came back with a bar of soap, toothbrush, tooth paste, a towel and wash rag. "Feel free to use the Jacuzzi tub or the shower, whichever one works best for you." He said as he turned on the television. He set an iPod on the nightstand right next to a small tube speaker, "There is plenty of music to choose from on this IPod, some R&B, as well as some meditation music. Find something that works best for you once you are in the bed and settled. I will be across the hall if you need anything else. If I am asleep before you, feel free to help yourself to anything in the fridge. Oh and if it makes you feel more comfortable, lock the bedroom door!" he screamed as he exited.

Ameesha immediately went into the bathroom. It was amazing just like the rest of the house; laced with a double sink vanity, Jacuzzi tub, the new age programmable shower, and amazing decor. His house had the comforts that any woman would love and it made her feel at home. Ironically, it didn't show any sign of a woman living or even being there. She ran a hot bath. He even had candles around the tub with a lighter stick and she made herself right at home. She still pondered how she didn't even know this man, yet she felt so comfortable with him... comfortable enough to even sleep with him. She thought about how wrong it would be for her to go there physically with Cantrell. He had pegged her to be some cute nerd or sexy librarian, but she actually had a Masters' degree from Freak'em University. She could take at least 8 inches down her throat and 12 inches deep in her vagina and asshole. Also, she wasn't passive, she liked to devour her toys, and she could make a 12" dildo completely disappear up her ass. Just the thought of what she should and could do to him made her horny along with his gentleman like ways, and the fact that he wasn't paying her any real attention at the moment. She got out of the tub, dried off, and laid in his bed naked. It felt like heaven, but she was by no means sleepy. She was horny as fuck and wished that she had her dildos and lubricant. She rolled over on her back and plunged two fingers into her pussy and pulled them out to look at them. She was tempted to send him a pic of her wetness like she did to the guys that she enjoyed teasing on the anonymous chat sites. She decided that she would really look like a typical whore if she did something like that, or worse she would alter his perception of her. A text message came through on the phone and it was Netta:

Netta: Did you make it home safe?

Meesh: I am safe, but not at home. I will elaborate in the morning.

Netta: Ok

Netta must have been drunk because her nosey ass

never let anything go that easy. Ameesha didn't want to sleep alone, she wondered if Cantrell was asleep? She unlocked the door and stuck her head out into the hall. She could hear him on the phone, and it sounded as if he was telling one of his homeboys about the fight at 321. She was just about to close the door when his daughter's room door swung open, she was busted.

"Why are you eavesdropping on my conversation?" he laughed.

"I wasn't eavesdropping sir, I thought that I heard a loud noise." She said.

"Maybe you heard the refrigerator slam? I had to pour me a glass of wine. I'm having trouble sleeping with you across the hall from me. I'm so used to having ugly female visitors, I don't know what to do with myself." He said sarcastically.

"How rude of you sir! You didn't ask if I wanted a glass of wine." She screamed.

He said, "I thought you were sleeping ma'am but here you take this one, I haven't drank from it yet, and I will pour myself another one."

"Actually, I'm not really a wine drinker. Do you have anything strong like tequila? I need something that will knock me out or I will be up all night being that I'm not at my own place." She asked.

"Yes, one of my partners left a little bottle of patron in my truck. I took it out when we were coming in, I will go and grab it." He said while walking toward the stairs.

As he scurried down the steps Ameesha yelled, "Grab a couple of shot glasses, I want you to take a shot with me."

Cantrell returned from downstairs with the bottle of Patron and two shot glasses. Ameesha was still standing in the hallway with nothing on but his t-shirt and this made Cantrell kind of feel that she was already his. Her round face and complexion reminded him of the female rapper Eve, but Ameesha had a more refined look to her. She had that ripe beauty; the beauty that she hadn't grown into yet while she was in her 20's; the beauty that he felt so privileged to have gracing his home on this night.

"If we are going to take shots, we should do it over a card game. Do you play tunk?" he asked.

She answered, "Yes Sir, I was the best in my dorm at tunk and spades. I used to be my son's fathers partner when we would play against his guy friends."

"Oh ok. Well I'm an expert myself, that means that one of us is going to be really drunk in the end (Cantrell chuckled). I will give you an out though, once you have had too many shots (which you will), I will allow you to do a dare if you can't handle another drink, deal?" he said.

She nodded her head in agreement. Cantrell grabbed a deck of cards out of the nightstand next to his bed and handed them to her to shuffle and deal. "Now before you deal the cards, do you play 49 and 50 is an automatic win as well as lowest hand?" Ameesha replied, "Of course fool, you aren't talking to no rookie." Cantrell picked up his cards and smirked, she picked up hers and sighed.

"Go on and pour you a shot boo," Cantrell dropped

two kings, two jacks, and a 10. "50 baby!"

Ameesha screamed, "You cheated you fucker, there is no way that I dealt you 50 on this first hand!"

"Woman take that shot and hush, this is only the beginning," Cantrell laughed.

A half bottle of Patron later, they both could do nothing but dares. He won a hand and dared her to twerk. To his surprise she hopped off of the bed, lifted the t-shirt, and gave him a 3 second ass show. When she won a hand, she dared him to kiss one of her butt cheeks, and he did so willingly. Finally, he dared her to kiss him, and she got one her knees in the doggy style position and kissed him passionately. Cantrell had a pillow on his lap hiding his erection the entire time that they were playing cards. He was so hard that it was starting to hurt as he continued to hold it down. The very next hand, she had 49. She laughed, and dared him to remove the pillow from his crotch area. Although he was embarrassed, he did as she had dared. To his surprise, she got back into the doggy style position, but this time she put her face down in his crotch. She started to nibble gently on his shaft through his boxers and laid a gentle hand on his on his stomach urging him to lay back. He was in complete shock, Ameesha had slid all 9 inches of his shaft down her throat, and just held him there for what seemed like two minutes without coming up for air. His whole body was stiff, and it felt as if she was stimulating his entire nervous system. When she would come up for air, she would go right back down slowly, all of the way down to the balls. Ameesha made it her business to work him slow. She wanted him to suffer and strain with pleasure. With a hand on his abs as she worked him, she could feel his muscles tense up with her every action. She had him straining and gripping the sheets just as a woman would who couldn't handle a big dick. Every time he tensed up as if he was going to cum, she eased off and just licked the stiff vein up near the head of his penis. She learned that move from an online tutorial. The instructor on the video said that the vein up under the head of a man's penis was like the clitoris on a woman, one of his true pleasure spots. She kept him in the space between straining to cum, and not being able to cum for at least 15 minutes. She was in total control and he was her puppet and toy while his body was her playground. She decided that she had come too far; he probably already viewed her as a loose, nasty, freak hoe, so she decided to add to his list of disgust. She gave his rock hard cock two good tugs with her hands, and she could have sworn that his soul exited his body through the hole in his penis. He let out a yelp like a little scared puppy, and then he came in levels; one big one that splashed the back of her throat, a second one that gave her a tongue full, and a small third one that she pulled up out of him as she licked him clean. She looked his shocked ass dead in the eyes, swallowed every drop that she had taken from him, and then tongue kissed him. He grabbed her in a bear hug and held her close as a person would do to a relative that they hadn't seen in years, or as a fighter would that was tired of getting hit. He was so powerful, but he was holding her tight as if he was afraid of what she would do next. Cantrell thought to himself, "She didn't just do me like that. I can't go out like this." He released her from the hug and pulled her t- shirt off. He began to gobble up her breast, making his way with bites and nibbles down to her stomach. Ameesha instantly had an orgasm. The touch of a man was so different than sex toys, or better yet an unmanly man. This man here was an alpha male. He held her by her hips in such a manner that she couldn't get away from his slippery tongue. He pulled her legs apart and plunged his tongue into her. She was in heaven and didn't even need any dick at this point; she was cumming with every ten licks. When he finally took his face out of her pussy and went to work on just her clitoris alone, something boiled up inside of her. It felt as if she had to pee, and as his tongue slid slowly across her pearl tongue, she released. Ameesha had never squirted before in her life. She honestly thought that it was a myth, but this man had taken her there with just his mouth. He looked up at Ameesha with all of her white and clear juices covering his face, and that made her even hornier. He climbed on top of her and inserted every inch of his manhood into her dripping wet pussy, and it was euphoric. This man somehow understood that she welcomed a pounding and trying to long stroke her to death would only make him bust fast. He made adjustments, he started to shove himself into her pussy from different angles, angles that she could have never emulated with her dildos. He finally found a sensitive spot in the top left side of her vagina, and he pounded her until she came twice. Her dildo never prepared her for a big dick with a curve. This was sexual bliss, her juices were flowing full blast, and his dick was the big spoon stirring her macaroni. The sound of her vagina's wetness interacting with his penis let her know that she was doing her job. She heard him whisper to himself as he was straining, *"My balls are even wet"*. She understood where he was coming from because she had juices running down the crack of her ass. He had won round two, but she had an idea that would end this love making session for good. She pushed him up before he could cum, laid him back, and sucked all of her juices off of his big penis. He almost looked afraid, he couldn't believe what was happening to him. Finally, she straddled him, and while looking him straight in the eyes, she inserted his slippery wet manhood into her asshole. As her hole adjusted and slowly slipped down each inch of his penis, she felt his body tighten up again. His legs were shaking and he was moaning in a high pitch voice as if he was going to cry. Right when Ameesha felt his testicles touch her ass cheeks, signaling that she had every inch of him in her hole, she thrust her hips forward just twice, and waited for the explosion. Cantrell screamed and then roared like a lion as he released everything that he had into her asshole, and he was done. She kissed him gently as she watched him drifted off to sleep.

CHAPTER ELEVEN

"*DATE NIGHT*"

Ameesha had never walked the Purple People Bridge before, it was one of the most amazing experiences of her life. The skyline, the city lights, and the view from the bridge was amazing. Watching the lights flashing on the boats and barges made the Ohio River seem more like the Hudson River in New York. Even though it was early fall and fairly warm out, the breeze from the river made it chilly on the bridge. Cantrell gave her his blazer because he noticed her shivering while trying to remain sexy in her thin green dress. She was terrified of water; she even hated to drive over water. Walking over water to her was like hang gliding off of the Grand Canyon, but the fear was arousing being that she was walking the bridge with him.

Cantrell laughed at her obvious fear. He used it as the perfect opportunity to grind on her huge behind. He hugged her from the back and said, "I won't let the water hurt you babe." He had been walking a few steps behind her, admiring her shapely legs and protruding backside. Her hips and cheeks swayed side to side like the pendulum of an old clock.

They had been dating for several weeks now, yet still the sight of her caused him to have an erection. He wanted nothing more at the moment than to bend her over the railing in the center of the bridge and fuck her senseless up under the stars without worrying about who could see them.

Ameesha's life had changed drastically since she met Cantrell that fateful and eventful night at the club. Initially, she had feared he would treat her like trash being that she slept with him on the first date; well technically she slept with him prior to the first date because their first date was breakfast and a walk the morning after they had sex. To this day she didn't know why she had given herself to him so recklessly and freely, but she didn't regret it one bit. It came as a surprise to her though that he clung to her instead of running from her. Most of the women that she knew swore that if you slept with a man on the first date, he would treat you like a cheap whore and would never entertain a relationship with you. Boy were they wrong! Cantrell had been nothing less than the perfect gentleman, actually he had been the perfected perfect gentleman. He handled her with extreme caution and care outside of the bedroom. Now in the bedroom, he had been punishing her for how she took advantage of him that first night. Ameesha chuckled to herself, she sure loved it when daddy punished her. He took being a gentleman to the extreme. Forget having a man open the car door for you, he always went the extra mile and would help her into the car as if she was carrying his baby. He did this every single time that they were entering a car. He had taken a photo of her to an artist friend of his and had him create a portrait from it. She wept like a baby when she walked into his bedroom one day and seen the beautiful artistic interpretation of her hanging on his wall. She really lost control of her emotions when she read the caption: *Love seemed like nothing more than a fairytale until I met you. You came into my life to be my woman, you did not try to make me your man, and I love you with all of my heart from that.* That statement hit home with her because most women tend to sleep with a man and then try to shape him into a comfort zone for their emotions and insecurities. They start trying to fix the man's life, becoming more of a mother figure to him than his woman. This becomes a compound problem because once a man begins to view a woman as a nag, or as a motherly figure, he will no longer be sexually attracted to her thus causing her to feel undesirable. Most women want to hold out on the sex for 60 to 90 days, yet they give a man an earful of nagging during that time period. They want to attempt to read him, tell him about all of their insecurities and heartbreaks from the past, and tell him about all of the bad things that they have heard about him as well as the signs and patterns that they will be watching for. No no no, not her. She was more concerned with giving him a mouth full of her vagina. She understood that her boyfriend wasn't her psychiatrist; his job was to love her, not heal her. In her opinion, if a woman needed healing, she needed to get that prior to getting a boyfriend or she would just end up running him off the same way that she more than likely did her previous one. The night that she had initially slept with Cantrell, she exhaled; she decided to leave all of the hurt and issues from her previous situations in the past and to just sit back and allow a man to make her happy. Ameesha had been receiving the royal treatment for being open and honest without all of the games. Even after sleeping with Cantrell on the first night, she didn't wake up the next morning giving some silly excuse for her whorish actions. She proceeded to act more like a whore. The way she rationalized it was that there were a lot of women sitting at home right now playing games with a guy that they had just met. Trying not to have sex, investigate him, seeing if he would call first etc. but here she was enjoying life with a good man. She had been dating this man for 80 days, and fucked him about 70 of those days, but she had just enjoyed a lovely dinner with wine at the Rib House with him on the 81st day. Whores don't get that treatment. Tonight she was walking the Purple People Bridge and wearing his jacket while he froze, so if a game was being played, she was winning. She was going to end her night with dick in her belly, and she was 100% confident that he would desire her even more as time progressed. She thought to herself, *"These women can play their games all they want, but Ameesha is done with games, and about to live her life!"* Ameesha didn't take the failed approach to dating a new man. She didn't pry into his business, or look at him through a microscope searching for flaws or inconsistencies in his actions, she simply enjoyed him. She didn't even think about building a future with him. Looking forward to the following day was all of the future that she needed. Social media helped Ameesha a lot. She used to ride that bitter "I hate men" bandwagon. She used to be a student of hurt women who gave nothing but bad advice in regards to dealing with black men. She was observant enough to realize that none of those women had men, nor did they get any male attention. She started to pay attention to this guy Mic Drop on Facebook who posted interesting articles, and sparked dialogues that offered honest male opinions. Ameesha truly learned to listen to men by reading those articles and posts. Now when men spoke, she listened. It was stupid to continue listening to women tell her about men, when she could simply just listen to   men   speak   on   themselves.

CHAPTER TWELVE

"COWARD TO CONFIDENT"

Morgan still couldn't believe that she had finally found a man; not sex partner or some guy to go out on dates with, but an actual man. Men of all shapes, sizes and colors pursued her endlessly, so her problem was never *getting* a man. However, finding a man that Prez would approve of had proven to be a lot more challenging. Thank god this wasn't the case with Darius, her brother had taken a liking to him. He wanted her to marry Darius because not only did he feel that he would be the best brother in law ever, he also felt that he would be a good man for her as well as a great father if they were to have children.

When Morgan initially met Darius in Atlanta, he seemed to have it all together. In hindsight, she realized that he had been hurt by multiple women before and his self-esteem had been destroyed. Due to this, he showed insecurities in ways that were similar to woman. For instance, although he was short with a chiseled frame, he considered himself to be little and pudgy. Since he done well business wise and had a lot of the finer things in life to show for it, he felt that everyone looked at him as if he were a nerd or cornball that hit the lottery.

In the bedroom, this man had been digging deep into Morgan's vagina as well as her soul. Here it was, almost a year since they started dating, and her vagina still hadn't adjusted to him! A long night with him always had her on pins and needles the next day because she was left with an open, air filled vagina that made a gross noise when she walked. He actually thought the shit was funny but there was nothing funny about walking by people and having them hear your vagina blow as if it was a damn trumpet. She didn't know if she was coming or going; he had her mind, body, and soul, yet he was still questioning himself about things as if she only gave him praise to be sarcastic. This made Morgan realize that in a lot of ways, men are just like women. They may not beat themselves up over an uneven skin tone, but they still held on to past hurt and esteem issues just like women do. She hated this about Darius because as a woman, she wanted a lot more confidence and cockiness out of her giant dick little man. Women love confident men, but he wasn't confident at all... well... until he started hanging out with that damn brother of hers...

Prez created a monster out of Darius! Somehow they ended up watching the NBA All-Star game at a grimy bar out on the Westside when a fight broke out. A guy swung on Prez over a woman and Darius knocked him and his friend out cold! Darius gained some street credibility behind it, and now the damn fool was driving to the projects by himself to play poker and spades on Friday nights with the hustlers. He was even fucking her differently! At first he would question his sex game saying, "Am I doing this right?" or "Do I do that right?" Now he was demanding blowjobs in the car, pulling over in the park, and fucking the shit out of her right outside on a bench! He would even come to her bar, pull her into the stock room, eat her pussy, fuck her senseless, and then dip without even washing off his dick. She loved that type of shit! They still had their love making days as well where he paid attention to every part of her body and was gentle with her. She appreciated getting the best of both worlds. What she loved the most was when he would lay her down on her stomach, nibble on her cheeks, and kiss her lower back. One day when he was fucking her from the back in his truck, Morgan could have sworn that she heard him say, "Bitch you love this dick! Your pussy is wet as hell!" Before she could even get angry, she felt his testicles slapping up against her clitoris. He was banging her too good for her to argue with him!

Outside of the bedroom, Darius had become more of a cut throat business man. Although he wouldn't admit it, Morgan believed that he and her brother were attempting to capitalize off the violence that was occurring in the Westside projects that was spilling over into the housing district as well. This had people afraid to buy or rent in the area and a lot of the owners were selling their homes for cheap just to get their families away from the chaos. A company that Darius funded, along with some white guys from Indian Hills, were grabbing up everything in that area for cheap. However, he never spoke on what they planned to do with it. Morgan wasn't abreast to everything that Darius was doing business wise, but she could tell that his new found street edge had him doing bigger and better things and making those clandestine mob like power moves.

Morgan really appreciated the fact that the new and improved Darius wanted to see Prez get out of the streets. He tried to get her brother to work with him but Prez knew nothing of hard work and labor. Darius ultimately hooked him up with a young, "square" women who owned a woman's clothing boutique in the Bond Hill area. Darius knew Angie for years, they were friends back in high school all the way up until she left for the military. He saw her out once at the Mid-Month Mixer when she had been discharged. She asked him about finding her a retail space for a boutique. She traveled throughout the world while in the military which put her in direct contact with clothing and fabric merchants all over the world. She was eager to bring world fashion to little old Cincinnati! Darius always admired her work ethic so he gave her and Prez a business loan to expand her shop into a men's and women's boutique that focused mainly on 1 of 1 rare pieces. He figured this would be a good business venture for Prez because he could afford to travel with her to aid in selecting good quality pieces. It wouldn't be hard for him to keep it strictly business either because Angie was a true nerdy chick: thick glasses, thin, and dressed with little to no sex appeal. She was definitely considered undesirable from a male perspective. Now Darius was right about one thing, the boutique flourished for the both of them, but thinking that it would be all business was a big mistake on his part.

Prez explained to Darius he initially felt that Angie was unattractive. He even went out of his way to have different women bring him lunch up to the shop, or stood out front while he was on break flirting with the women that walked by. He didn't want her trying to come on to him and then have to turn her down. That would have made for an awkward work relationship. Angie started calling him "Lil Thirsty", and mocked how his tongue would hang out of his mouth women would come in to try on clothes.

One day, a white and gold cat suit came in from Thailand in their clothing shipment. Angie asked Prez if he liked it. He shook his head and twisted his face to say not really, but left the door open saying that maybe he needed to see a woman with a nice body try it on. After having lunch with some chick that he had met over the weekend; he walked into the shop just as Angie was walking out of the dressing room with the cat suit on. She had removed her glasses and let her hair down. He was stunned at the fact that she was amazingly beautiful! She asked if she looked okay in it... he was speechless and couldn't respond! Under all of the loose clothing, the woman had small, sexy, curvy hips like the ones Halle Berry had, along with a tight little Jennifer Lopez booty. She looked thick in the cat suit, yet she couldn't be more than a size 2. He could even see her firm ab muscles through the material of the suit. Just staring at Angie's frame gave Prez a rock hard erection. He looked down to see if she would pass the Boomerang test, and sure enough she had pretty and perfectly manicured toes. He couldn't stop himself from walking over, grabbing her up in a bear hug while saying, "Woman where have you been hiding all of this?" She informed him that she wasn't hiding it, she was just a well-traveled woman that knew how to be sexy while fully clothed.

It was he who couldn't see sexy outside of half-naked women, and she was right, he was as shallow as they came. Prez couldn't stop staring! Angie said, "Ummm, your little gun is poking me sir! Put that little thing away before I teach you how to use it."

Prez laughed and said, "You are too small boo butt, I'd break you in half!"

Angie ran her tongue across his lips in a manner that almost made him cum and said, "Well lock the door and let me see what you got."

She did all kinds of sexual and freaky tricks on him that she had learned while stationed in Taiwan. People were knocking on the door, but it never broke her sexual rhythm, she had him in so many different holes that he couldn't tell if it was in her mouth, ass, or vagina, all that he knew was that he had never felt anything like it in his life! That was 3 months ago and now Angie was living in Prez's house, 3 months pregnant with twins.

Darius laughed at himself... he had won both ways. He didn't want Prez in the streets anymore, and to get him away from that life he knew that he would need a good woman to do it. Angie previously expressed to Darius how hard that it is to find a single man in Cincinnati that didn't want to use her. She had grown tired of men that wanted to use her car and stop by her fucking place of business while driving it needing gas money. Darius killed two birds with one stone. He placed his good friend Angie in the hands of a man that he had grown to trust with his life, and placed that man in the hands of a woman that would bring out the good/God in him. Now he had Prez's finances, street connections, along with Angie's contacts to the foreign markets.

CHAPTER THIRTEEN

"THE PERFECT PARTNER"

"Get off of my ass boy, you are acting like a horny dog!" Ameesha screamed.

Cantrell laughed and hunched Ameesha's leg like a little dog. She snatched away and ran from him, well she didn't actually run she cute stepped because running in tall and sexy heels was almost impossible. He couldn't believe his luck. How many men came across a woman who was amazing in bed, good looking, and wasn't immediately emotionally or financially needy? Not that he was cheap, and it wasn't that he was cold hearted, but sometimes women could be too much too damn early. He definitely wanted to give her the world and his heart in due time, but as a man, he hated when women acted as if he owed them something after they slept with him. He felt that was a creative form of prostitution when a woman claimed to be independent before sex, but wanted to be dependent afterwards. He preferred that a woman ask for what she wanted up front because if it was something that he wasn't willing to give, he would just pass on the woman and sex altogether! Ameesha was different though, very different. She seemed to be one of those women that had been schooled by her big brother or a good father. She didn't show the usual signs of insecurities and past hurt; she actually came across as over confident, and that was her sexiest quality. She never questioned herself, nor did she try to force him to label what they were doing thus causing more insecurities. For weeks on end now, day in and day out she was sexing him senseless. The woman never ran out of tricks in the bedroom! It seemed that she was a totally different woman every time they had sex. What he admired most about her though, was that she wasn't in a rush to make him a presence in her son's life as some of the women that he had dated in the past were, nor did she try to get into his daughter's life. She would always joke with him about it too, stating that he would have to go through a lie detector test and a police interrogation if he wanted to meet her son. Her words were, she could handle a man walking out of her life, but any man that was going to walk into her son's life would have to be prepared to stay. Children should never have to feel like they have been abandoned by an adult that they had grown attached to. In his eyes, she was the definition of a good woman; she was that woman that every man needs by his side.

Ameesha never tried to pry into his business, but when she saw a chink in his armor, she gave him input. She noticed that he had two large dump trucks on the side of his building with perfectly operating tilted beds. She asked him

136

who did they belong to? He informed her that he had inherited them from his uncle Roscoe, but never had a serious use for them outside of hauling trash and the construction debris from the remodeling of his building. One day she called him out of the blue and asked for his social security number. Initially he thought that she was doing a background check on him, and he was hesitant. He gave it to her anyway because they had already slept together and he could tell that she was really into him. There wasn't anything in his criminal history that would make her question their dealings at this point. A week later, to his surprise, she started him a construction waste disposal and debris removal company. She named it, *Trellways Debris Removal LLC*. She had him transfer the titles of the trucks over into the company name, and found him two drivers who were willing to drive for a percentage of the company verses getting paid a salary. This made it all good for Cantrell because the drivers would work hard at building the company, and he could sit back and get a percentage of the profits with no effort. This woman was so wonderful, she pulled some strings and slid his company in as a subcontractor for some highway work on I-71. All he had to do was get bonded and insured, but she had already set him up an appointment to do that the following week as well. She observed him; she paid very close attention to the things that he migrated to. She had compiled a list of his interest and recorded ideas that he would sometimes throw into the air but forget to investigate further, and she would ask him how could she help him make those ideas a reality?

This was his first time actually being around a woman

that made him want to see and be with her all of the time. Even when he didn't have time to be with her, he still felt a strong need to be around her. He also found himself wanting to get closer to her son. It wasn't like he hadn't ever seen her son because he had met her in traffic on several occasions and the boy was in the backseat. He had several play fights with the kid and talked the usual male to young male trash with him, but he hadn't actually bonded with him. He now yearned for the bond, because he yearned for all of her and wanted to reciprocate the good that she brought into his life by being good to her prize possession.

CHAPTER FOURTEEN

"MOVING IN SILENCE"

Ameesha knew nothing of Cantrell's street ties and it was getting harder and harder to work around her. He was at his homeboy Flee's house getting his pack ready for distribution when she called and asked of his whereabouts. He told her the truth and said that he was at Flee's helping him to mount his new television to the wall. She left work early and was just checking on him, but wanted to see him briefly. About 30 minutes had gone by, just as he finished putting the last two bricks in a backpack to give to his homie, Ameesha came knocking on the door. She had his favorite dish, chicken tikka masala from the Indian spot, and she had grabbed some for Flee as well. This put him in a very odd predicament because he had to text all of his loyal workers to tell them not to come to the spot and to just hold off until he called. He didn't like holding a pack longer than an hour or two, and Ameesha caused him to have to sit there dirty for nearly 4 hours. She didn't mean any harm, she was clueless, but Flee kept texting him and asking why couldn't he just tell her the truth so that they could move how they usually do? Telling or showing her how he really got down was not an option, not right now anyway. What kind of example could he be to her son if he revealed to her that he sold drugs? He could already tell that from her upbringing, she would equate him being a hustler to selling drugs to children and being a senseless murderer. He had seen square women act like that in the past when it came to some of his other friends from the hood. Cantrell felt a sharp pain in his shin and almost screamed out loud! Flee had kicked his leg from under the table signaling that he needed to get Ameesha out of there. Cantrell snapped back into reality and said, "Babe what do you have going on for the rest of the day?"

"Nothing much, why what's up?" she replied.

"Well, Flee and I need to run to the hardware store and get a few more things. Can you go down to the market and get some red snapper for me? I have a taste for that brown stew snapper that you cooked for me awhile back." He explained. He knew that she would jump at the opportunity to head to his house and cook.

"Of course I will go babe, anything for you. By the way, do you mind if I bring Lil Lonzo over with me? My mom has a church function to attend tonight and Lonzo hates those things so I won't have a sitter." She asked.

"No problem at all, my home is the little man's castle." He handed her a small wad of 10 dollar bills, and said, "Grab him a toy or game. I just want him to have something to play with when he comes over."

"Thank you sweetie!" She said as she gave him a kiss on

the cheek, grabbed her purse, and headed out of the door.

As soon as she was outside of the door, Flee went in on him! "Damn bruh, I like to see people all in love and shit, but her square ass is in the fucking way! I'm not about to get myself jammed up because you want to duck and dodge your new girlfriend! When it's time to shake and move, it's time to shake and move, and you need to make her respect that. Mannn you need to refocus so that we can get this money. Why don't you just lie to her and say that you have to go out of town or something when you know that it's time to bust a move?"

Cantrell could do nothing but respect what Flee was saying, yet the thought of lying to Ameesha didn't sit well with him. Keeping her in the dark was one thing, but lying to a woman who hadn't done him any wrong was just foul in his eyes. He vowed to Flee that he would have her on or off board by the time the next move came around. Flee shot him that twisted lip look that symbolized disbelief. Cantrell had no comeback. All that he could do was shake Flee's hand, make his calls, and proceed to finish up the job.

CHAPTER FIFTEEN

"MERGING MY WORLD"

Ameesha felt bad lying to Cantrell. She knew that she had a baby sitter but they had been dating for 3 months now and it was definitely time for him to meet Lil Lonzo. She was trying to think of a way to set up the meeting, but with both of their busy schedules, a lot of the time they ended up hooking up late after her son was already asleep at her mom's house. Today was a blessing for her, she was cooking for both of her men under the same roof. As Cantrell entered the garage and exited his car, he smelled all of the Jamaican seasonings and spices that she used to cook brown stew. He also could hear her son terrorizing the house and her yelling at him to stop whatever it was that he was doing! As soon as Cantrell opened the door to the house, he and Lonzo, who was only 7 years old, had the most intense stair down ever; you would have thought that they were about to draw guns on one another like they did in old cowboy movies. Lonzo walked over to his mom and grabbed her leg, but never broke his stare. Cantrell told him to get away from his girl as he walked over to give her a hug. Lil Lonzo punched him in the leg and said, "Get off of my mama!" then all hell broke loose! Cantrell got down on his knees and he and Lonzo boxed it out over Ameesha. Cantrell was getting the best of the boy, but Lonzo landed a good one on the side of Cantrell's head! Cantrell played hurt and laid on the ground holding his head. Lonzo was a little animal, he showed no remorse. He hopped on top of Cantrell and hit him with a barrage of punches! Cantrell went for a headlock as both of them proceeded to wrestle around the room. The only thing that stopped the battle was Ameesha standing there holding two plates of scrumptious fish and buttered broccoli, with fried potatoes and onions. She broke up the fight by saying, "Will you two crazy boys wash your damn hands so that you can sit down and eat?" That started another competition in itself! Now it was a race to the sink to wash their hands!

This was always Ameesha's dream; having a strong black man around her son that he could really like and take to. Although Lil Lonzo knew his dad, he was murdered when he was just one years old. She thought about how a lot of her friends wouldn't approve of, or date a guy like Cantrell, but Ameesha was learning more and more that there is good in everyone regardless of their background or upbringing. She realized that a lot of guys from the streets tend to come from broken homes where they were forced to be the fathers in their families when they were just boys; or they had their minds impregnated with the idea that they weren't shit, and never would be anything more than that. That causes a young

143

man to have something to prove and to try to seek validation from the outside world. This is the concept that causes men to go out and sell drugs, rob, and kill; all in an attempt to prove that they are "The Man." If someone could have just redirected their vision back into the household, they would understand that they don't have to do all of that just to provide a good life for their woman, children, and families. A lot of women could have a good man if they were to curb his desire to show off and seek outside validation by redirecting his energy into what it takes to build an empire; starting with securing his own household. When home is taken care of and there is no pressure to bring in an overabundance of material, a man starts to realize that extras are extra and not a need. When a man's philosophy of life switches from what or how much he can show outsiders to what can he add to his family, he then becomes a strong black man.

Feeding her big man and little man made Ameesha feel so womanly. In today's society, women have to do manly things, or pick up a man's slick. It's often rare for a large majority of women like her to get a chance to just step back and be the woman that they were meant to be.

After everyone ate, the men got right back to tussling. Next thing she knew Cantrell challenged Lil Lonzo to a game of NBA 2K. While they headed back to play the game, Ameesha used that time to sit on the soft recliner and dig into her new book *Confessions of a Scorned Baby Mama* by Marina J. She heard that it was a great read and had been eager to get started on it. She was reading for over an hour when she listened to see what her guys were in the back doing. She peaked into the bedroom and found both of them sleeping…

Cantrell was asleep on his back while Lonzo slept perpendicular to him with his feet on top of Cantrell's face. She now had the answer to her question about how Lil Lonzo would take to Cantrell, he obviously enjoyed him. She turned to hurry back to her book while she had some quiet time when she heard, "Meesh."

Cantrell was calling her name, she turned around and said, "Yes babe."

"I need a favor babe. I have a childhood friend who has a girlfriend that is very rough around the edges; she is good peoples though. I know it isn't your job, but for me, could you mentor her? Help her like you helped me? She has her own money, she just needs direction and someone on her side that will help her execute." He asked.

How could she say no to the man that has made her life complete. "I would be honored babe. Any friend of yours is a friend of mines. I will treat her like a sister." She expressed.

He could barely whisper the words, "Thanks babe." He was too busy drifting back off to sleep.

CHAPTER SIXTEEN

"HOOD AND UNPOLISHED"

Ameesha could not believe that she was on the infamous Tot Lot! When she agreed to meet Cantrell's friend Sylvia, she had no clue that she would be in a hood spot that looked like a clean crack house. The furniture was old and outdated and there were liquor bottles and ashtrays everywhere as if it was a hangout! The shades were broken in a few places indicating that someone stared out of the window like a lookout. Ameesha had been trying for hours to get through to the young woman, but everything that she tried seemed to fail.

"It kills me when someone says that I can't run the streets forever. What the fuck else am I supposed to do?" Sylvia said.

Ameesha stared at Sylvia with the *"What the fuck?"* face. She had been talking to the girl for two hours straight and she still hadn't gotten anywhere. This chick was a thug just like some of the men from the hood. She seemed to have more thug in her than Cantrell! All she ever talked about was fucking up bitches and bitch ass niggas. The interesting part about her was that she was video vixen bad; she had the slimmest but curviest shape that Ameesha had ever seen. Her face and skin were flawless and she dressed like a lady: red bottom heels, fitted jeans, and a cute, red, waist cut Michael Kors leather jacket. It was impossible to believe that a young woman this attractive could talk like a guy in a maximum security prison. She admitted to Ameesha that she had stabbed both women and men, shot a few dudes, and even hinted at committing a murder or two. Normally people like her scared Meesh to death, but Cantrell said that she was family, so she knew that there was nothing to fear.

"Why can't I be a hit bitch like the chicks in the movies? You know, take niggas out and get paid to do it?" Sylvia said with conviction.

Ameesha finally snapped and said, "No god dammit! You are going to tell me what the fuck you are good at, not now, but right fucking now!"

Sylvia burst out laughing so hard that it caused Ameesha to laugh too even though she had tears of frustration in her eyes. Sylvia said, "Ok, damn Meesh Meesh, get those Wal-Mart thongs out of your crotch! I'm trying to come up with something geesh. What about party promoting and throwing concerts? Is that a career?"

"Yes; promotions, marketing, and event planning is big business. It's a lot of work behind the scenes from what I hear though, but I think that your little bossy ass could do it.

Let me ask you this, how much capital do you have?" Ameesha asked.

"Upwards of $70,000... I never spend the money that my male friend gives me; I stash it all for a rainy day. You won't catch me out here fucked up and having these hoes laughing at me." Sylvia said.

Ameesha let out a long sigh, "Look Sylvia, you put waaaayyyyyy too much thought into what other people think of you. Learn to focus all of your energy on your man, your life, and your finances. If you don't learn to tune people out, you will always be a part of the rat race, going around and around on the hamster wheel playing keep up. Learn to be your own motivation; stop letting beating out other women who look just like you be your motivation."

Sylvia thought about what Ameesha said and it made sense. She needed to act like these hating hoes didn't even exist. "So where do I start?" Sylvia asked with enthusiasm.

"I have no clue, but what I do have is some contacts in that field. I will gather some information for you and meet back up with you later on in the week." Ameesha said. Both women nodded to one another in agreement...

CHAPTER SEVENTEEN

"THE BOND OF SISTERS"

Lunch at Mama J's soul food wasn't going to be good for Ameesha's waist and hips, but the smell of fresh macaroni and cheese as well as cinnamon filled sweet candied yams filled the air like an expensive fragrance. Ameesha set up a meeting between Sylvia and Morgan, who was a younger friend that she met back when she attended St. Ursuline Academy. Life had pushed them in different directions, yet they both still ran in the same circles of people so it wasn't hard at all to get in contact with her. She had known for a while now that Morgan inherited a club from her father. A lot of their mutual friends frequented the place, and from what she heard, it was nice!

The smell of the soul food alone explained why there was always a one hour wait to be seated. You would think that with all of the money the place made they would have upgraded the furniture by now. They had the same old red and blue plastic looking tables with matching chairs. The inside was jam packed! It took her over two minutes to locate her old friend Morgan. She spotted Morgan over in a corner with her head down staring into a laptop. She gave Sylvia a tap, signaling for her to follow. Ameesha gave Morgan a gentle tap on the shoulder, Morgan stood up and gave her a hug yelling, "Hiiiiiii girlie!" Morgan extended her hand to Sylvia, and Ameesha intruded: "Sylvia this is Morgan, owner of the nightclub Fire on the Westside, and Morgan this is Sylvia. Sylvia is a novice but hungry promoter looking to bring some different acts to the city, as well as introduce some creative party themes."

Morgan looked Sylvia up and down. She looked to be about business; all black red bottom pumps, tailored gray business suit with the knee length skirt, and her jet black curly hair was pulled back into a ponytail that hung down her back. Just by the look of her, Morgan knew she could use Sylvia on her team. Women need to see examples of other women working in a club who are sexy yet classy at the same time, and Sylvia was just that. Morgan held a high standard at her club. Week after week she had to turn women and men away who believed that the more an event cost it made it upscale or warranted dressy attire. Morgan broke the ice by asking, "So what types of acts are you thinking about bringing if I may ask? We can't bring most hip-hop acts here because their images conflict with the concept of the club."

Sylvia spoke up without hesitation, "There will be no hip-hop acts unless we were going to do Lauryn Hill, Mos Def, Common, or someone of that nature; I was thinking more on the R&B side, like Trey Songs, Mary J Blige,

Teyanna Taylor etc."

Morgan shook her head in approval. "Acts like Trey Songs cost a lot of money don't they? How would you pay the artist if you couldn't manage to sell enough tickets? I wouldn't want an artist not getting paid for hosting an event at my club and effect my future endeavors. The reason being is I'm thinking about throwing a huge party Jazz Festival weekend and having several different artists host it."

"Let's just say that I'm a trust fund baby. Money will not be an issue, and I too have plans for the future. To achieve those plans, I must fulfill any and every contract that I sign even if I lose a little." Sylvia answered.

Ameesha was wowed by Sylvia's response! All of her coaching wasn't done in vain.

Morgan thought to herself, *"This young woman sounds serious as cancer and if she has her own money to bring the acts, how could I ever lose a dime? This could only help to bring attendance up and give my club national exposure."* The waitress interrupted the conversation by asking what everyone wanted to drink and if they were ready to order. In unison they all said, "3 wings, greens, and macaroni." They looked at each other and chuckled!

"Now back to the matter at hand... If Ameesha says that you are family, you are family to me. So Meesh, do you cosign this young lady?" Morgan twisted her head in a sexy hood rat manner, stared Ameesha in the face, and waited on her reply.

"She is my protégé and my man's little sister. I back her word with my word and my wallet." Ameesha answered with confidence.

"Well, we are now the triad of sisters! Give me a hug sis!" Morgan opened her arms to Sylvia and they both hugged as if they were old friends. Morgan changed her facial expression to one of anger and turned to Ameesha. "Now about this man of yours Ameesha... when do I get to meet him? It's not fair that Sylvia knows him and I don't what type of sister shit is that? I haven't heard about you and a man since... (Morgan paused)."

"You don't have to pause, and you are right. I hadn't been with a man since Lonzo's death. I honestly thought that I would never get over that situation, but Cantrell has made my life worth living again." Ameesha explained.

"We need to arrange a triple date! I can meet your man and you can meet mines... Well, as soon as his short, buffed ass gets a break from work." Morgan said with excitement.

"Who is he? What's his name? Where did he go to school? Did you make him take an aids test before you screwed him? I need answers!" Ameesha said in her school girl voice.

Morgan burst out laughing! "Well my office in the club has a kitchen in it. Maybe we ladies, including you Sylvia, can invite our men to brunch this Sunday. Are you with or seeing someone Sylvia?"

Ameesha shot Sylvia a quick look. Sylvia replied, "No not at the moment. I had a bad break up with him last year and I've just been giving myself time to heal."

"That's understandable... we all go through it once, twice, or thrice." Morgan replied. "Sylvia, why don't you come by the club tonight? Its ladies night and you can check out the set-up, meet my team, and we will talk more about artist, timing, and strategy."

CHAPTER EIGHTEEN

"CHEATERS"

Bleed eyed Rae Lynn walking towards the coffee shop on Elm Street. She had a body like no other and by her walk alone, he could spot her from a mile away. Renzo's lame ass had him one right there! Ever since Renzo did that little bid in Arizona for trying to mail some weed back to the city, he had been feeling himself. Somehow while he was sitting in the county down there he came up on a serious plug. The plug was so real that they were already in Cincinnati waiting when Renzo was released. They plugged him with everything, literally, from coke, heroine, regular weed, to Kush. He had the city on smash. Even dudes with more money still had to buy from him because he had out of town prices right here in the city. I guess that's why it made sense that he bagged Rae Lynn. He was just a lucky square for real, and she damn sure was a square. She was always the little weird Performing Arts type of chick; the nappy fro, spree shooter boots and a screen hoodie. Even though she dressed and looked weird as fuck, no one could deny that she had a fat ole' ass! She would never talk to anyone when she walked by Hard 2 Knock Shoppe back when it was down on Race Street. She never even turned her head or acknowledged anyone. Word was that Renzo bagged her by acting as if he was interested in seeing some play that she was in. They say he bought all of her tickets and had everyone that he dealt with attend. I guess weird chicks liked lames that were interested in weird shit as well because her big booty ass fell for the weak shit. She was claiming him as her man just a few weeks later. That was over five years ago though and they were still together so that lil' shit must be good to him. She was every bit of 23 or 24 now, but she had dropped that weird look and was now a bad motherfucker on some low key and plain Jane shit.

Bleed was parked right in front of the coffee shop, leaning on his van, hoping that she would notice his preppy boy sweater and Khaki outfit as she passed him to go in. Weird chicks loved the school boy look, and lucky for him, today he wasn't rocking his signature black hoodie and dark denim; he was dressed like an Ivy Leaguer. He could see from a distance that she had done away with the fro and now had a fresh bob, cut high on one side, but hung shoulder length on the other side. It seemed like every time he saw this girl she got thicker but her waist got smaller! Her dark complexion and skin were flawless, and her bright white teeth shined on her face like a diamond necklace does on an all-black t-shirt.

"Damn little Rae Lynn, I see you ain't got that fro no more." Bleed said while laughing.

"Excuse me? Do I know you from somewhere?" she asked curiously.

"Well, I don't know you personally but I used to see you walk by Hard 2 Knock Shoppe back in the day when I would be shopping rocking your serial killer boots, with your back pack resting on top off your big butt." He explained with sarcasm.

Rae Lynn gave him a shy smile and said, "I know I was a mess back then… Don't judge me!"

"Na, I'm not judging you at all, I thought that you were fly back then and I damn sure think that you are fly now." Bleed expressed.

"Well thank you sir that was very nice of you to say. I'm sorry that I never noticed you trying to get my attention. I had the lowest self-esteem back then. When I would walk by guys, I would just look down at my shoes because I felt that they were laughing at me." Rae Lynn stated in an embarrassing tone.

"That's hilarious, because the entire time we all thought that you were just stuck up!" he said while laughing.

"Hold on, wait one minute! I know who you are… You are Sylvia's dude. I took Karate with her at the dojo in Clifton a few years back, you used to come up and watch sometimes. How do you deal with her? She is one angry woman!" she asked.

"Nah she is cool peoples, she's just misunderstood. But since we are finally talking after all these years, can I say something without you judging me?" Bleed asked to avoid indulging in a conversation about his woman.

"Sure, I'm a big girl now, I can handle it." She

said.

"Your ass is stupid fat... and that is all." He said in a sincere tone.

Rae Lynn started laughing! She admired his bluntness, and to be honest, she was pissed that she had over looked such a tall cutie back then. She would love to have had him instead of Renzo's no swag and no personality having ass. She also remembered over hearing Sylvia telling a girl in class about how she always felt him in her stomach when they would have sex. Even though Renzo was decent in bed, she was intrigued by the thought of having dick in her stomach.

"Boy gone somewhere with that! I'm not trying to be arguing with psycho Syl over your black ass, so don't be trying to get your little holler on. Go on home to your light skinned wifey." She screamed.

"Come on now, don't act like that. A conversation ain't never hurt nobody, besides, what she don't know won't hurt, you know how that old saying goes. Seriously though Rae Lynn, I've been watching you for a while now, and yeah that ass has gotten fat, but what I have really been peeping about you is how you don't get caught up in all the hype. I know your dude Renzo gets money, but I don't ever see you trying to stunt with the red bottoms and expensive handbags. For real, that's what turns me on about you. Asses come a dime a dozen, but a woman that's not trying to blow dozens of her man's dimes on bullshit is a rarity." He explained.

Rae Lynn pondered what Bleed said, and he had made a correct assessment of her. She spent the money that Renzo gave her on things like books, organic foods, yoga classes, and wellness seminars; she preferred to put money into herself instead of on herself. She knew chicks that rocked $2000 outfits every day, but every curve under their clothing was manufactured. They spent more money on girdles and spanks to go up under their outfits than she did on her actual outfits. She preferred to blend in while in public but put other women to shame when she got naked for a man.

She smiled and said, "That's a great assessment sir; I'm glad that you noticed. I always thought that you guys were into those chicks with the pulled in waist and costume makeup. Like, when I go out from time to time, I be thinking that I look nice, my ass and tits sit right in my clothes, everything on *fleek*, but men don't break their necks to try and holler at me. I can be standing next to a clown looking chick who looks like she is about to pop open like a can of biscuits and guys stay running up on her, buying her drinks and basically acting thirsty for her. I be out there thinking that I have shit all wrong."

Bleed thought about what she was saying. He couldn't deny that it was true, but he saw it differently. "I don't think that it has anything to do with how the woman looks, I think it has more to do with what her appearance implies. When a man sees a woman who appears to have gone out of her way to look inviting, he views her as approachable and open. Some men even equate wild make up to wild sex. If the woman looks wild, she is wild, if that makes sense?"

Rae thought about it and it made sense... a toned down woman doesn't look inviting, but shit she liked attention too! Not saying that she would cheat on Renzo, but a man going out of his way to get her attention still made her feel good, that's just one of those womanly things that men never realize.

"You seem to have stuff all figured out Mr. Bleed, but I have a question for you: if you know all of this about women and you are so polished, why did you mention Renzo's name when you tried to talk to me? Isn't it a rule or something that a man can't say another man's name while attempting to get a girl? My brother used to say that all of the time when I was younger." Rae Lynn asked.

Bleed snapped back instantly, "You are correct young lady, that is definitely the rule but it doesn't apply to this situation in particular."

"Why is that?" she asked.

"Well, I only gave you a compliment and spoke on my observations of you. I did not try to holler at you." He explained.

Rae Lynn raised her eyebrow, "Oohhhhh, ok I get that! I jumped the gun or made an assumption. Well excuuuuuussee me sir, it won't happen again. I was under the impression that you were going to ask me out to dinner or take me to get a massage or something. I heard Sylvia say that you did that for her, and I've never had a professional massage, the thought of it sounds amazing. Sucks to be me I guess. Renzo isn't taking me to Columbus with him to the Rich Daddy concert that he is throwing because he is mad at me and you just shitted on me, so I guess I will just sit my shitty ass in the house and read a book. Well you have a nice evening sir, but thanks for the compliments".

Bleed chuckled and said, "Woah woah woah shorty hold up, you are moving too fast. I don't disrespect anyone's relationship and I didn't know that the lane was open for my plane to take off. Shit if you are free, I'm free, just tell me a time and place to meet you. Would you like for me to book us a couple's massage at Serene & Sensual spa and do dinner afterwards? Can I buy you a drink? I mean just tell me what it is that I have to do?"

Rae Lynn laughed, "Now that sounds a lot better 'Mr. I Ain't Trying to Holler'! Yes, I would love a massage and dinner. Don't judge me either by the way that I'm dressed before the massage, judge me on what I'm rocking afterwards."

They exchanged numbers and Bleed vowed to text her as soon as he confirmed the time for their massage. Watching her walk away made his balls hurt! He felt his manhood stretch far down his leg and seemed to damn near touch his knee! He felt sorry for Renzo, if he got a crack at Rae Lynn tonight, she definitely wasn't going to want him anymore. Word on the streets was that he paid good because he couldn't fuck good. The man rule that she didn't know was, if you ever get a hold to another man's piece, you make sure that you give her a good disrespectful fuck. Women love to be disrespected in the bedroom and he had a long disrespectful piece of dick for her.

Bleed sat on the couch watching Sylvia get dressed. She looked amazing! Her hair was long and blond and hung down the back of her fitted purple dress and she was rocking some black thigh high boots that laced all the way up her leg. He loved seeing her in those boots; they made her look sexy and bow legged. She had grown into her body and was a far cry from the little girl that he once knew. She was still petite, but she was what most men would call stacked. She still had the same baby face, she just carried a more serious look in her eyes.

"What do you have going on tonight babe?" he asked.

"Me and the girls are going down to the Mixx Lounge for sushi. Can you believe that I'm going to try sushi?" she asked.

"Yes I can believe it. I've noticed the change in you ever since you and Trell's girlfriend started hanging out. You have gotten all bougie on a nigga, so yeah, you eating some bougie sushi sounds just about right to me." Bleed said while laughing.

Sylvia did a spinning kick, stopping her foot just an inch shy of his face. He grabbed her ankle, kissed her foot, and said, "You aren't crazy! I brought you into this world, and I will take you out."

She mimicked the kicking motion while gently letting her foot slap his face, "Don't make me hurt you Bleed! I don't play all of the time." They both had to laugh at her attempt at being serious with him.

"What are you getting into tonight though? Are you going down to that damn house joint in West City to play spades and poker?" she asked.

"Damn that's a good idea. I was going to sit here and watch a game or something but spades sounds better. Gambling always takes my mind off of the bullshit. Judging by your outfit, you are going somewhere after sushi anyways, so I might as well hangout." he said.

"Yeah, one of Morgan's friends is having a birthday party at the club tonight. Its royalty themed and you know purple symbolizes royalty." she expressed.

"I'm jealous! All that ass in that dress, don't make me have to come and shoot the club up because some dude was staring at you to hard." Bleed said.

Sylvia laughed, "No matter how hard they stare babe, I'm sitting this lil booty on your face at the end of the night."

Bleed rubbed his hands together like Stevie J while licking his lips. Sylvia stood in front of him and gave him a gentle peck on the lips while grabbing his manhood, "Love you babe. I will wake you and him up when I get home." As soon as Sylvia walked out of the door, he grabbed the bags of new gear he had hidden in the coat closet. It was time to get dressed for his date with Rae Lynn. He purchased a simple khaki blazer a while back, and he had a really nice white Versace printed button up to rock up under it. Both his shirt and blazer had been tailored to perfection and the ice blue, stone washed 7 Figs jeans that he was going to wear were tailored as well. Together it all made for a very expensive looking ensemble. He topped the outfit off with some caramel colored Tom Canady dress boots. At his height, he looked like an NBA player at the press conference after a big game. His choice of cologne for the evening was *Million* by Paco Rabanne; he heard someone say that with this cologne you were guaranteed to score. He chuckled to himself, "I hope this statement proves itself to be true."

Rae Lynn stared at her naked body in the mirror; all of the yoga, weight training and healthy eating had done her body well. She had her mother's thighs, backside, and hips, but she also had her dad's skinny genes. Her dad was only 5'3", and she seriously doubted if he weighed 90 lbs. soaking wet. She inherited a very low body fat % from her dad, and this is what contributed to her waist being abnormally small in comparison to her thighs and hips. Rae Lynn loved the attention that her appearance got her from men. Growing up with a bunch of insecurities and then blossoming into a vixen felt like hitting the lottery to her. Unlike the stuck up girls who turned their noses up at a guy, she liked all men's attention, except for the ones at the gym. Guys at the gym were pest and they would ruin a woman's entire workout just by constantly trying to holler at her. Men sometimes didn't understand that just because a woman likes a little attention, it doesn't mean that she wanted to fuck. Rae Lynn had been with her boyfriend Renzo, and only Renzo for over five years. She had no desire to cheat. She was loyal as they come to her man, outside of just some casual flirting here and there. Now, tonight though, she was going to allow Sylvia's boo to take her out and show her a good time. She didn't feel bad at all about it either. Renzo wasn't taking her to the concert that he was throwing in Columbus and he didn't even have the decency to leave her a few dollars knowing that she lost her check card. This made a date tonight with Bleed all the more possible. She be damned if she sat in the house alone and stressed over what Renzo's ass was doing in Columbus. She prayed that Bleed wasn't the over aggressive type because him getting some was out of the question. For one, he and Renzo knew each other, and for two, his chick Sylvia was crazy as hell. She heard so many rumors of murders committed by Sylvia directly. She even heard that it was her, not Bleed that killed those two dudes by the shoe store on Hopple Street.

Rae Lynn used to be afraid of guys like Bleed. When she got with Renzo, he seemed to be a total square. Well he still was a total square, but now he was just a square with money. That's all that he had too was money; his sex was just average and he wasn't really over the top sexy or cute. He also really couldn't converse outside of typical street stuff which could take its toll on a girl too. The thing that she hated most about Renzo was that he was a liar; he just lied about everything for no apparent reason. He could get caught red handed in the car with a bitch with his pants down, and he would still say, "I ain't with this bitch". That burned Rae Lynn up because the truth helped her to relax and have a peace of mind. No matter how bad the situation was, she wanted the truth, because what she hated more than a man doing her wrong was being kept in the dark. She snapped out of her thoughts, realising that it was time for her to get dressed. Her outfit for dinner was to die for and the sweat suit that she was wearing to the actual spa hugged her body as if it were a cat suit. She was so eager to just get out, be flirty, feel sexy, and just be a girl again. She had been cooped up too long being Renzo's little chick. She was going to give Mr. Bleed a serious case of blue balls tonight and she was already giggling at the messages that she knew she would be receiving from him in the morning. She loved it when men begged... After he dropped her off at home tonight, or by morning, he would be offering everything but his soul to taste her goodness.

Serene and Sensual spa was one of Bleed and Sylvia's

favorite places. The streets can take a toll on a person causing all sorts of tension and stress. A good rub down was always a good stress reliever, and he and Sylvia lived in the place. What he liked most about it was that it was out on the East End, away from all of the hustle and bustle of the city. He also knew that if he took Rae Lynn out to eat on this side of town, and hopefully to a hotel, he wouldn't get busted. He loved the fake waterfalls that created the relaxing nature sounds, and the lighting always made him feel relaxed and sleepy. The fresh flowers and plants that were in every table, the fruity fragrance of the place as a whole, and the relaxation music made the experience worthwhile. Oh how he hated bullshit music. Lyrics like "Suck my dick bitch I'm a boss" didn't register to him as good music. He preferred instrumentals or Jazz for the most part.

As he followed closely behind Rae Lynn, he thought about what she had said earlier... don't judge me on what I am wearing to the spa, judge me on how I look after the spa. But she looked damn good to him before the spa. She had on a gray hoodie and sweats, but the sweats hugged her ass and hips as if they were tights, they were only loose from the knees down. He couldn't even imagine what she had in the overnight bag that she was carrying, but he knew it was going to be sexy as hell. He had never heard of Rae dealing with anyone but Renzo so he knew that this was a one shot deal if he wasn't a perfect gentleman. He made a pack with himself to not allow thirst to overshadow his finesse.

The woman behind the counter at the spa asked for his id, she handed it back and said, "Welcome back Trevor and Sylvia," while handing them both a sign in sheet. Bleed's mouth dropped and Rae Lynn burst out laughing. Bleed leaned in and whispered to the receptionist in a very serious tone, "Sylvia and I aren't together anymore, and can you remove my information from the system all together." The receptionist stuttered, "Uhhhh, yes sir Mr. Bledsoe, no problem." Bleed looked back at Rae Lynn, she was still giggling. He hoped like hell that the receptionist didn't ruin his chance, because if she did, it would be the last thing that she ever ruined. He snatched Rae Lynn's clipboard and said, "Let me see if you checked yes to any std's." With lightning speed, she snatched his off of the table and said, "Nah negro, let me see if you got them bumps," they both starting laughing. The masseuses walked out from the back and gave each of them an inviting welcome. They were escorted through the door that led to the locker room areas. Bleed's favorite masseuse, Gloria, shot him a 'That's not Sylvia' look, and he felt like a piece of shit. He was so caught up with the thoughts of potentially sexing Rae Lynn, he had forgotten that everyone in Serene and Sensual were on the name to name basis with Sylvia. He hoped like hell that the receptionist or Gloria didn't mention any of this to Lu Ann, Sylvia's nail tech. Sylvia didn't talk much around people, but her and Lou Ann were gossiping buddies. Lou Ann knew and told everyone's business! He hated to wait for Syl during her appointments with Lou Ann; they were both motor mouths, chattering nonstop. If Lou Ann got wind of this, she would tell Sylvia for sure, but he was too far in to turn back. Actually, he planned on going at least 10 more inches in. In the locker room, he removed his clothes and hung them neatly on a hanger inside the locker. He normally kept his boxers on during a massage but he decided to free ball this time because his manhood was rock hard and thirsty for some of Rae Lynn's water. He hoped that Rae Lynn would be looking during the massage when it came time for him to roll over on his back, the sheet would surely be sticking up about 12 inches from the table. He was rock hard just imagining how she looked taking off her clothes in the room next door. He wished he could get a sniff of her perfume, or better yet her cookie. He so loved the smell of a fresh and clean vagina, it brought out the animal in him.

There was a slight tap on the door; it was Gloria, alerting him that they were ready for him in the massage room. He looked up, grabbed his belongings, opened the door, and followed Gloria to the massage room, where he found Rae Lynn already standing inside. The masseuses said in unison, "We will give you two a few minutes to discard your robes and get under the sheets. We are starting face up today, so we need both of you to lie on your backs." Bleed opened his robe and let his pride hang, knowing that Rae Lynn would look. My God! Rae Lynn thought to herself while acting as if she wasn't looking. The rumors were true, this man hung 3 times longer than Renzo, and even in the dim light, his penis looked to be at least a half inch thicker than his as well. A voice in her head told her that she was staring, so she decided to flip the tables back on Mr. Bleed. She slowly removed the belt to her robe, letting the robe drop to the floor. His pride lifted up as if it was on a crane, and it now poked straight out in front of him aiming directly at her.

"You like?" she whispered while giving him a 360-degree spin so that he could take in the rest of her body.

"Heeeeeeeellllllllll yeah, I don't think that I've ever

seen a body so sexy, not even in a magazine." He said with amazement.

The little woman had hidden hips and a lot more ass than her jeans from earlier or her sweats revealed. He couldn't see too well because the room was dark, but she seemed to be several inches wider in the hips, and her waist looked as if it belonged on a skinny woman's body. He felt a little pre cum drip from the tip of his penis. A slight knock on the door broke up their little staring session and they both almost broke their necks trying to rush up under the sheets before the masseuses entered the room. Bleed's imagination was running wild; he wanted to stick his tongue in her mouth, grip her ass with all of his strength, hug her from the back, massage her feet, and kiss her toes… "shiiiiiittttt!" He thought to himself. Let me just calm down and enjoy this massage.

"This man must be packing at least 10 inches," Rae Lynn thought to herself. She pondered what it would be like to sex him as she allowed the masseuse to work her magic.

After paying for an amazing massage, Bleed sat in a comfy chair thinking about Rae Lynn. On top of being attractive, she had an amazing spirit. Even though she was technically stepping out on Renzo, she wasn't making Bleed feel as if she were only hanging out with him to spite him. There was no way in hell she was getting away tonight without giving him some of that, but then again, just being with a beautiful soul and gentle spirit on a night where he would have just been home alone was a blessing. He told himself to just chill. He was reading a Sports magazine for what seemed like an hour when a voice said, "I'm ready sir."

He looked up to find Rae Lynn standing there in all of her glory. She had on a fitted, but not tight, nude colored body suit that had a v shaped split in the front revealing portions of her ample breast as well as her pierced navel. God himself had to be holding the fabric over her nipples because there was no way that the outfit could hold them in; they looked like small and perfectly round melons. It seemed that if you were to stand close enough to her, you could look down inside of the v shaped opening and see her vagina. The leopard print, 6 inch heels set it off though. They had her legs and hips looking heavenly. He hopped up from the chair and took her bag. Before he could throw it over his shoulder to carry it for her, she reached in it and grabbed a red clutch purse. The clutch seemed to add more fire to her outfit, being that her manicured nails were red as well, they were a perfect complement to the clutch. As they exited the spa, she leaned in and said, "Now how do I look?"

"I can't lie, you look mighty scrumptious." Bleed said while licking his lips.

Rae Lynn batted her eyes while giving him a seductive smile and said, "I like that... Even though I was aiming for fuckable." Bleed laughed. He felt his temperature rising and wondered if she was just kidding or was it an open invite. As he opened and held her car door, he took the opportunity to take a few deep breaths. The little voice in his head started talking to him... "Calm down, don't rush anything. Earn her goods and don't sit around all night wondering if she is going to offer them to you or not."

Dinner at Eagle's View restaurant was amazing. Bleed had never eaten there before and neither had she. The service there was world class and the chef came out and spoke with each patron before preparing their meals so that the dining experience would be a unique one. The high pricing didn't reflect in the décor; the inside looked like the cheap restaurants down in Gatlinburg, Tennessee where everything was made from logs. The walls, tables, chairs, and even the bar were all made of logs. A person had to be into wood working to respect Eagle View's fancy log construction. It probably wouldn't excite the average person that much. Now what the patrons were paying for was the view. The restaurant sat on the back side of Mt. Adams, overlooking the Ohio River. The entire back side of the restaurant was glass so that you truly overlooked the city while dining there. You were privy to seeing Cincinnati's skyline, bridges, boats, as well as Kentucky's Newport on the Levee area, along with the light show that came with such architectural splendour. There was even a huge deck that hung over the cliff. The deck had a huge fireplace on it so that patrons could still dine on the deck even when it was chilly out. This made sitting across from such a beautiful woman like Rae Lynn even better. Staring into her slightly slanted eyes, and watching her luscious and full pink lips move had him aroused beyond his wildest imagination.

"So Trevor, if I can call you Trevor, I have a question for you." Rae Lynn said while sipping her wine. "What turns you on the most about women?"

Bleed thought to himself for a second, "If I had to choose one thing, I would say her smile. There is something about the way that a woman smiles that moves me inside, even when the woman isn't attractive."

Rae Lynn gave him an intense stare and said, "I thought that you would have said something like ass or tits."

"Nah, I see ass and tits all of the time, but in this era of angry women and contorted facial gestures a beautiful smile is rare." He said. Rae Lynn nodded her head in agreement.

Bleed flipped it on her and said, "So let me ask you the same question. What do you find most attractive about a man?"

"Physically, I'm into his style of dress. I'm really into men that step out of the box when it comes to throwing it on, that's why those Tom Canday boots that you are wearing caught my eye. I want to fuck them." They both laughed and she continued... "My main thing though is his ability to be honest. I love honesty, and I hate men who lie to women just to sex them. I'm a woman that hates to be kept in the dark, so even if you think you will hurt my feelings, still be honest with me."

"Boooooo! Women always say that and then flip out on you when you tell them the truth, so I don't believe you." Bleed said sarcastically.

"We aren't discussing what you believe sir. I just told you what I like." She said in a serious tone. Bleed couldn't do anything but respect that. "With that being said, I need an honest answer from you that has been on my mind since we crossed paths earlier... With a woman at home who is as beautiful as Sylvia, who gets her own money, because I've heard rumors that she owns a club now, who, when in public, dresses to impress, and who most men would kill to have;

why are you here with me in an atmosphere conducive for cheating?"

He simply said, "The answer to that is easy ma'am. I'm a man, and men still lust beautiful women even when they have one at home already."

"Hmmmm, I thought that you were going to come with the typical male excuses like her sex is whack, she gets on your nerves, she's not adventurous enough, you know?" Rae Lynn expressed.

"Nah it's not that at all, I can honestly say that Syl is perfect from her conversation to the bedroom. If I had to find a flaw, the only thing that I would be able to say is that she can be hot headed at times, and that's only when I have provoked her." He replied.

"That's deep... so you are saying that even perfect women get cheated on?" she questioned.

"Unfortunately, yes." he replied.

"So as a woman, when I start to feel ugly and undesirable when I see messages from my man to other women calling them cute and sexy; or if I get word that he has been spotted with another woman, it doesn't mean that I need to step my game up or that I am doing something wrong as a woman; it just means that he is a hoe?" she asked.

Bleed laughed and replied, "No, he's not a hoe, he is a man. Men don't look at cheating the same way that women do. Most women love to have an emotional attachment to one man, and only a handful of women can sleep with a man without becoming emotional. When a woman cheats on her man, 9 times out of 10 she is reaching for or giving up something emotionally along with the sex. That's why when a woman who is being taken care of cheats, it's normally with a man that she has talked to too much. It's always with some guy that she works with, goes to school with, interacts too much with on social media, or worse, the dude whose number that she excepted while she was mad at her man etc. The interaction gives men a chance to play on a woman's hurt emotions, men sense a woman's hurt. Men on the other hand, we will screw a chick for simple reasons like she walks sexy, her ass is 1/2 inch fatter than our woman's, the way the woman's lips look, how sexy her outfit is etc. Shit I screwed a chick once because she had pretty feet, it's just the animal nature in a man that gives him a beastly attraction to women, but we don't leave emotion everywhere that we lay like women do though."

His honesty made Rae Lynn squirm, and for the first time since they had linked up, she pondered sexing him. She had never heard a man break down cheating in such an articulate manner.

"So you think that you know women I see. That's cute." She said while giving him a seductive look.

Bleed gave her a sinister smile and replied, "I've been dealing with women from all walks of life for as long as I have been able to pick up a phone and call one. It isn't that I know them per se, it's just that I've noticed patterns. I'm also notorious for eavesdropping when women talk, so I have had a front row seat at times into a woman's mind. Sometimes when I'm bored and don't have anything to do, I will go sit in Shonda's salon down on Central Avenue just to listen to the ladies chatter. But on to you... It's now time for you to take the hot seat ma'am. With a man like Renzo at home who makes sure that you are good, why are you here with my good for nothing ass?" he chuckled.

Rae Lynn gave him his same sinister smile and answered, "Good is perception. Men sometimes think that bags and shoes are the only requirements when taking care of a woman, but women are emotional and spiritual to the core. If a man isn't giving his woman anything emotionally and spiritually, he is not caring for her realistically. A woman can't hug a bag when she is cold, or vent to a shoe. Do you know how disappointing it is to have something deep on your mind that you want to share with your better half, and he comes home at night wanting to talk about how much money he made that day or who is hating on him? Do you know how lonely it feels when you just want to sit by the river and talk, but he texts you to say get dressed because he is taking you to the club with him and his homies? It's even worse for me because I grew up artsy an eclectic. I have the soul of one of those weird punk rock girls, I have just managed to look the part of a street dudes wife by being observant of other chicks in my position; I've even watched Sylvia. Sylvia dresses sexy not slutty, from what I hear she doesn't gossip, she doesn't talk about you to other people, and she's never anywhere being thirsty for attention. I admire her style, you won with her."

Bleed pondered what she said and responded, "Damn, that's deep Rae, and you just made me reflect on my own relationship. I've probably dropped the ball as well to be honest. I do a lot of the things that you just stated to her.

Thank you for setting me straight, because I too can get caught up in myself at times, while neglecting her basic needs. Geesh, if you were mines, I would kiss you right now woman."

"We are spiritual beings sir. The Stars marked this date and time. Look at the moon, it's full and the stars are in full display. They remind us of the billions of opportunities that await us if we open up and let the universe in. Kiss me sir, I am open to a kiss." She said.

Bleed leaned across the table and kissed Rae Lynn's lips, they tasted like strawberries. She placed a gentle hand on his cheek letting him know that she enjoyed his tongue. He felt electric coming from her soul, now this was a Bad Bitch.

"I have a few more questions sir before we follow whatever path that the stars have marked for us tonight. First, did you bring any condoms, and if not, why?" asked Rae Lynn.

"To be honest, when we talked earlier you expressed how much you were into health and wellness and I just couldn't see a woman like you carrying around a disease. Also, when a man really likes a new woman, he wants to give her his all and condoms can sometimes limit a man's erection. A woman once told me that you had to take the condom off to touch a woman's soul, so if I was blessed with the opportunity to bed you tonight, the back of your vagina wasn't going to be good enough for me. I would have needed to touch your soul." He said.

"That was heavy sir; I feel as if you just licked my pussy, conversation is the best foreplay. Well let me say this, I too understand the connection of raw penis to a woman's soul, and if I'm going to cheat on my man, I want an experience not a fuck. If I'm not seeing stars, I've wasted my juices and simply gave a man outside of my own the opportunity to say that he just fucked me. I rationalised allowing you to bed me raw as well if we did have sex tonight. The way I see it though is that Sylvia is fucking crazy. I've seen what she could do at the karate tournaments, so I told myself that if you had a disease or had given her a disease, you would be dead already and we wouldn't be having this conversation anyway." She expressed.

Bleed almost spit out his wine! All that he could say was, "True True."

"Ok sir this is the million-dollar question, are you ready?" she asked.

"Yes!" he replied with the upmost sincerity.

"If I were standing naked in front of you right now, what would be your first move?" she asked.

"Without question, I would lick the crack of your ass." He replied.

Rae Lynn squirmed in her seat, "Why my ass sir?"

"Well, I look at it this way, if I lick your ass and you still kiss me afterwards, I know that you are feeling me; if I lick your ass and it turns you off, I still win." He said.

"How is that still a win?" she said while staring directly into his eyes.

He explained, "If you are turned off and never spoke to me again after today; anytime that I saw that scrumptious ass of yours walk by from here on out, I could pride myself on having tasted it."

Rae Lynn laughed and said, "Real nigga shit! Well can you get the check sir because I've been eyeing that nightstick in your pants since the spa and I have been very eager to make you and it see the stars."

"Say no more babe, say no more." He said and requested the check.

To Bleed's surprise, Rae Lynn didn't want to stay at the hotel that he had reserved; it was a 5 star, Epic hotel down on the river just in case she did want to have sex. She wanted him to find the cleanest motel instead, the kind where you could park right in front of your room door. Upon getting into his truck, she stripped naked, and began playing with her pussy. The splashing sound that her fingers made going in and out let him know that she was extremely wet and slippery. He was catching hell trying to search for a cheap motel and at the same time watch her little show. She seemed to have forgotten that he was there; she was totally consumed as if she was acting out some sort of fantasy in her mind. He thanked god for expensive wine. He finally found a motel, so he drove west to Harrison, Ohio where he was sure that they wouldn't be seen by anyone. Neither of them needed that drama. Looking at her golden and naked body had him totally gone, he couldn't get to the room fast enough. As he exited off of I-74 to the Rybolt exit, he pulled into the Quick Sleep motel. It looked like one of those creepy truck stop motels that are always in serial killer movies. It even had the truck scale and diesel fuel station in the same parking lot. This place was only fit for crystal meth addicts and trailer trash prostitutes. The receptionist only charged him $19 for the room. That was a far cry from the $1500 that the Epic on the Banks wanted. When he got back in the truck, to pull around to the back of the motel to their room, Rae Lynn finally spoke, "I always wanted to get naked in the car and walk totally nude into a cheap motel room, and just give a strange man all of my goods. I've had this recurring dream/fantasy ever sense I started dating Renzo. He is so scary and cautious though; staying at a motel like this would be a no no for him. He would be so worried about someone trying to kidnap us or something that he wouldn't even be able to focus on me."

"Well rest your mind with me babe, nobody is kidnapping me or you." He said in the most assuring voice possible.

With a sensual whisper, she said, "I know..."

Watching Rae Lynn walk to the room totally nude with just her heels on had him awe struck. This woman defined sexy, sex, sex appeal, attractive and seductive. Her vibe alone pulled on his dick like a magnet. He couldn't get the motel room door open fast enough. The room smelled musty and of cigarettes. All of the furniture, including the bed and comforter were old. Bleed wasn't used to staying in no dump like this, but Rae Lynn didn't seem to care and if this is where she wanted to make love, he didn't care either. She walked right to the bed, grabbed a pillow and put her face in the pillow while arching her back high as hell. Her ass was enormous, and then she did that thing... The thing that drives all men crazy... She reached around grabbing both ass cheeks, spreading her pussy wide open, making her hole all his. He saw that little line of pussy juice stretch across her wide spread pussy lips alerting him that she had that stupid gushy wet stuff. He barely had his pants down when he stuck his head in, breaking that line of wetness and entering her slippery universe. Rae Lynn was going wild, she had insisted that he leave the blinds open so that the moonlight and stars could shine in. She definitely made a case for the rumor that weird and darker women had good pussy. He was only giving her half of his dick, and she was losing her mind. He had Renzo's piece calling him daddy. As he stared down to watch his rod go in and out of her sticky wet pussy, he admired the gushy cum that appeared on his dick during every exit stroke. He was stroking her with no hands at all, just standing tall, while shoving heavy dick in her. He wondered how much juice she really had, so he used his finger to scoop up some of her wetness. He plunged his soaked finger into her asshole, and just like he thought, she creamed his dick. This sent Bleed into a lustful rage! He grabbed hold of her waist, and began giving her all of his manhood, and he felt himself breaking through a different wall with every stroke. He had fucked her blind and she was probably so dick drunk by now that she didn't even know where she was. He realized that he couldn't let that happen, she wasn't about to pass out and forget this dick down that she was receiving. He picked her up with one arm, sat on the edge of the bed facing the mirror, then sat her seemingly lifeless but ready body down on his shaft. He wanted her to see what he was about to do to her as he began to thrust his fully erect penis up into her stomach. He only lasted 10 to 20 more pumps though; watching Rae Lynn's beautiful body in the mirror and actually seeing his dick all up in her stomach, all while having her lean back on his shoulder as if she were a lifeless fuck doll screaming,

"Bleed! Ohhhhh please baby!" was just too much for him. As he busted off into her guts, he looked out the window and felt as if he were a rocket taking off into those stars...

CHAPTER NINETEEN

"WHEN YOU WANT WHAT YOU CAN'T HAVE..."

"Why can't I stop thinking about her?" Bleed repeatedly asked himself while sitting in his truck waiting on Fred to return from Ali's with their fish and fries. Ever since his initial date with Rae Lynn, he found himself wanting to be with her more and more each day. It was something about her clueless and innocent personality that had him stuck on stupid... not to mention her dripping wet pussy. They had been sneaking and seeing each other for over a month now, and he found himself getting angry on the days that she couldn't get away from Renzo so that she could see him. Bleed looked at himself in the rearview mirror, laughed and thought, "I'm actually having a sucka attack." He couldn't go on much longer having to share Rae Lynn with Renzo, something had to give.

He could get Fred to kill the nigga, but he figured taking a life over a female could bring him nothing but bad karma. He could start robbing and extorting the nigga, but the fool had money, and he could only get that shit off for so long before Renzo ended up putting money on his head. The days of pressing weak dudes were over. There were too many grimy shooters running around nowadays that would kill for just a few bands. Bleed heard the notification tone go off on his phone, it was Fred sending him a screenshot of a convo from that social media group Team No Hoes. It was a thread of two women arguing over Renzo. One posted a pic of a $5000 bag that he allegedly purchased for her, while the other one posted a pic of some money in a gym bag that he must had been keeping at her house. This was all too much for Bleed, that clown didn't deserve Rae Lynn, and he was going to see to it that he didn't get to have her for much longer.

Bleed had been riding around looking for Renzo all day. He finally peeped him standing in front of the hairdresser/barbershop on Vine St. He couldn't believe what he heard... his Lil homie Cha Cha called him and said that Renzo had just posted a picture of him with $250k laying on the bed, and allegedly bought a $5000 bag for a $2 whore. It's funny because he never had any beef with Renzo, and he never wanted to rob him because Renzo always stayed in his lane. Well now it was obvious that the character was feeling himself a bit, and Bleed figured that it was time to get him before the police got him. He glanced back at Renzo, he was standing out there with his chess poked out as if he had really earned some stripes out here or something. Bleed put his gun in his waist, zipped up his hoodie and hopped out of his truck.

"Renzo my nigga, what's been popping homie? I hear shit have been real sweet over your way, and I'm happy for you. I wish that I could say the same thing for me, but it's ugly over my way. My girl came in the house yesterday telling me about some big ass expensive bag that you bought for that tramp Tyesha who be down on Linn St. She talked about that damn bag so much, that I had to agree to buy her one. You know I'm just like you, we will do anything for our girls, anything for family you feel me? So what I came to rap to you about was that I need one of those bags for my girl, and I was wondering if you would be willing to help me?" Bleed said sarcastically.

The two fake goons who were standing with Renzo started to ease away, leaving Renzo to face Bleed all alone. Renzo wanted to shit his pants, but he knew that if he showed fear in public everyone would come for him as if he were a goldfish in a piranha tank.

"Shit man, I'm fucked up too. I'm trying to sell that 550 right there back to the dealership as we speak. I can't lie, I was getting it for a minute, but my shipment got intercepted. Now I'm stuck with the loss and no connect because my people are afraid to move." Renzo explained.

"Listen here bitch ass nigga, I ain't trying to hear that shit! You didn't buy a whore a $5000 bag just two days ago, and you're broke today. Stop playing with me man before I shoot you in your face right here in front of everybody." Bleed said as he stepped closer to Renzo.

Renzo looked Bleed in the eyes, and knew that he was

dead serious. He definitely didn't want his girl Rae Lynn, who was inside of the barbershop to have to see him on the ground leaking blood.

"Ok man look, it isn't that serious. It doesn't have to come to pistol play, give me until tomorrow and you can have your girl come down here and pick the bag up from my girl's hairdresser Shay. It will be down here by 1pm, I give you my word on that." Renzo pleaded.

Bleed extended his hand and said, "Thanks my nigga, and by the way, I heard what you are paying for them whole ones and how many that you are getting in. I am not trying to rob you, but what I need you to do is sell a couple to my homie Bang from up on Harrison for the price that you are paying. He told me how much you be charging him, so he is willing to let me make the extras and not you. I give you my word as a man, this is not a robbery, you and Bang will do business as usual and he will just be sliding me my cut, do we have a deal? Or do I have to pop you right now while your girl is watching?"

"Nah man, I got you." Renzo said while shaking in his boots. "Now can you just go bruh? You are making a seen."

Bleed extended his hand to Renzo and the two men had them an agreement. As Bleed walked away, Renzo thought to himself that he just inherited all of this drama by buying a girl a bag that wasn't even his woman. He felt like a fucking fool!

CHAPTER TWENTY

"HE BRINGS OUT THE BEST IN ME"

Sylvia stood in front of the mirror in her room admiring her body; she had thickened up a lot over the last year. She loved her new butt, it wasn't big, but had just the right amount of poke out. Her breast had grown an entire bra size from an A cup to a B-C, yet they still sat up nice and perky. She was trying to decide what to wear to the club tonight. She didn't know if she should look sexy to fit in with the patrons, or if she should dress business casual. She had tons upon tons of clothes, some still brand new. She didn't want to pop up as if she was trying to show up anyone, yet she didn't want to look shitty either. She eyed a light blue romper, still in the plastic hanging from a hook on the backside of her closet door, and she knew that she had found her outfit. She had worn it once to dinner with Bleed over a year ago. It was too big then but she still rocked the hell out of it. Her new curves would fill it out perfectly now. She had some red Giuseppe pumps that would go right with it too, making for a toned down, but ultra-sexy look for the evening. All she had to do was accessorize properly and she would look elegant.

Sylvia sometimes wished that Bleed could be by her side on occasions like this, but his reputation preceded him. No one but her saw any good in Bleed. Club and bar owners hated him because he was rumored to have killed a kid in Grover's Pub down on 5th street. Even though he was never questioned about the murder, the rumors alone cast a shadow upon him. She even felt like she couldn't take Bleed to simple things like a friendly brunch with the girls. The second that someone recognized him, things would go from sugar to shit. She never minded it much when she was younger because everything that she did was hood; but now that Ameesha had been showing her different things, she really would have loved to be able to enjoy those things with Bleed. Even Cantrell advised her not to introduce Ameesha to Bleed. He didn't need her to know that side of him for real, and Sylvia respected that.

Sylvia heard a knock on the door. She wondered who the hell it could be being that she had just moved to this place. It had to be Bleed knocking, no one knew where she lived but him. But he would have called first so it couldn't be him, she thought... She threw on some sweats and a t-shirt, walked towards the door and said, "Who is it?"

"It's me bae! I left my phone in Speedy's van." Bleed replied.

She opened the door excited! Bleed was standing there with an Edible Arrangement and a bag from Saks. She took the fruit basket, while kissing him gently. "Thanks bae… you can be so sweet at times. What's in the bag?" To her surprise it was a pair of silver Louboutin's that would go great with her outfit for the night. "Oh my God they are beautiful! What made you get these?"

Bleed laughed and said, "I know what you look good in and I believe that a man who takes care of home will always have good luck."

She gave him a playful punch to the head and said, "Yeah, but how many homes are you taking care of nigga?"

He snatched her up and put her in a headlock. "Don't start that shit, don't play with me. Seriously though, I just put a bag with some money in it down in your storage bin in the basement of this building. We just had to kill that fool Renzo, and the cops are all over us because the beef is public. I don't want them to come for me and I have anything worth taking in the vicinity. My alibi is tight though, I went to Urgent Care and told them that I was burning during the time that it went down. I was still there when the shooting came across the news, so I should be straight. I won't be using a phone for a few days just in case they try to track me, but if push came to shove, I will just be here reading and relaxing."

Having Bleed there consistently would be awesome, she thought. He never really wanted to live with her because he didn't want his drama to come her way, but what he failed to realize was that she probably could protect him better than he could protect himself. She had registered guns, and her Krav Maga training taught her how to disarm a potential threat within seconds. The way that most street guys held a weapon made them easy pickings for a woman with her training background. Now, what she wanted him around there for the most was to help her chose artist to bring, and to point her in the direction of some people that could do some street promotions for her. He was a lot more in tune to the streets than she was nowadays. She wanted to ask why did they kill Renzo, but she learned that to ask is to know, and knowing was never a good thing if you weren't involved. She was pissed that she was on her period, because she would have gotten her some of Bleed's good loving before she went out to the club. Bleed broke her train of thought....

"How did the meeting about the promotions thing go boo? Do you think that you will be able to break bread with this Morgan chick? I remember her dad from when I was a youngster, he was a real gangster. He was a real serious dude that got to the money but would slit a throat or pop a top in a heartbeat. She has a brother named Prez that's a wannabe. Their pops left them everything; the club, some money, some property etc., and that fool still wants to play the streets. I really hate dudes like that; they hustle for the rep, not out of necessity." He said.

Sylvia couldn't believe that Morgan came from a hustling family. She seemed to be clean cut, square, and professional. "She didn't seem street at all to me when we met. She seemed proper and square."

Bleed squinted his eyes before saying, "If I recall correctly, her parents sent her away to boarding school or something. She wasn't raised around her knucklehead brother, so she probably is square."

That made sense to Sylvia. Morgan was a hood square which wasn't a bad thing at all. In her eyes, women like that always had City Hall connections, and knew of ways to get around certain paperwork issues.

Bleed looked at her with a very serious face and said, "To be honest, you and her should make a great team. She hangs around a lot of highly successful black women who have a hard time finding a man due to their success and sheltered upbringing. I've heard those types of women talk, and they think that every guy that didn't go to school with them or doesn't work with them is a bum. Her club stays packed full of those types of women, and a lot of them go home drunk and alone at night. My homie Suave said he met a chick like that once at Home Depot. She saw him loading up his truck with some drywall and she asked him if he did marble counters? He told her yes, so they exchanged numbers and he agreed to come to her house after work to give her an estimate. He said he doesn't even remember discussing any work when he got there, all that he remembers was wine and some good unexpected sex. The chick had some serious money too, with connections out the ass. In six months she had sent him so many clients that paid top dollar, he had ended up paying for her and him to take a trip to Aruba. Women like that long for decent men in their lives, they just need someone to connect them to the world that exist outside of their comfort zone. You can be that person. Whatever you throw at her place rather it be a concert or an event, let me know, and I will get hood cats that handle their business in real life to suit and boot up, and help to get yall numbers up!"

"Wow, and to think I just thought that those bitches were stuck up." Sylvia said. Bleed burst out laughing.

See that was the thing about Bleed that made her pussy wet. He wasn't a dumb ass negro, he was just caught up in the hood. He was very good at manipulating both sides of the fence and he always gave the best advice. She figured she would keep all of what he said in mind as she got dressed for her big night.

CHAPTER TWENTY-ONE

"CLUB FIRE"

Club Fire was nice! The walls were covered with metallic wall tile that you would see in places like Vegas. The flooring was wood, with some sort of shiny black stain that caused it to shine just like the walls. There were about 5 or 6 medium sized VIP booths. Sylvia guessed they were for people who purchased full bottles of liquor. The tables in the booths seemed to match the metallic look of the walls as well and each booth had a crescent shaped red or black leather sofa.

Sylvia was very impressed! She could clearly see that a lot of money had been put into the place. As she glanced around the room though, it looked like more of a sorority event. The only men that were there you could tell the women probably went to school or worked with. Sylvia thought to herself, "How could you throw an event or concert in a place like this and not have any ballers running around?" If she were to throw an event here, she definitely wanted the football players and polished street guys to be in the building. Hell, they didn't mind throwing their money around. This was true from clubs in Houston all the way to clubs in New York. The DJ was to die for though! He had a constant flow of danceable R&B hits flowing back to back including *Touch Me Tease Me* by Case, as well as the *One More Chance Remix* by the Notorious BIG. Everything about the club was top shelf and upscale. The bar itself was constructed following the same theme as the rest of the club, topped off with a solid black granite counter. Everything behind the bar was mirror and the mirrors reflected the beauty of the club. Sylvia had never seen an actual bar that big. It was a full circle around a huge mirrored post in the center of the building. It had at least 10 registers that would make for spacious serving for up to 15 bartenders. Sylvia was reaching down into her purse for some cash to purchase a glass of wine, and when she looked up Morgan was standing behind the bar as if she was ready to bartend.

"What's going on sister sister?" Morgan said while extending her hand to shake Sylvia's from across the bar.

"Trying to buy a damn drink sister sister..." Sylvia said while extending her hand as well.

"What are you having?" Morgan asked.

"I'll take a glass of Riesling if you have it." Sylvia requested.

"You are in luck! I have what most call liquid ecstasy, it is Pogue Riesling. It's been known to cause some happy endings if you know what I mean?" Morgan hinted and they both laughed. Sylvia almost slipped and said that her man was waiting at home to receive a happy ending when she got in.

"Put that money away, it's no good here! Let's have a seat over in the corner away from the speakers and discuss your vision for these concerts and events." Morgan said as she grabbed a bottle of wine and two glasses. She motioned for Sylvia to follow her to the corner booth. Morgan sat down and poured them both a glass. "So how do you like the club? And we are sisters so feel free to be honest." Morgan said sparking the conversation.

"I love the club! I see every dime that you have put into it and there are a lot of dimes. I honestly don't see you maximizing your return though. I've been in hood spots that had a lot less class and decor, but a lot more patrons at the bar with wads of cash in hand." Sylvia expressed.

Morgan sighed, "I know… it seems like the more that I uphold a standard of class for the place, the less men seem to attend. I get emails every day from my female patrons saying, 'Where were all of the men last night?' It's hard for me because I know mostly white guys who don't really party, so inheriting a black club has been a gift and a curse for me. I do turn a profit every month, it's not a huge one after paying my aunt to manage, but I do make some profit."

Sylvia smiled and said, "I honestly can solve the men problem for you in the short term: see women like you are in tune to the salary earning, corporate, degreed men, and that's perfectly fine. But there is a large portion of men who do well for themselves in other arenas. For example: I have a homeboy named Derrick who owns a car lot that all of the hood guys buy their cars from; I have a dude named Marcko that owns a highly successful tattoo business. I know a guy named Fred that DJ's all around the country, he was even the back-up DJ for Trigger Gunz last tour and they did 20 shows in Europe alone. See guys like them have money, cars, homes, take care of their children, and are intelligent, yet they may have never set a foot on a college campus or even filled out a job application."

Morgan took in what she was saying and in no way could she disagree. Men like the ones Syl just mentioned wouldn't even register as a catch to most of the single black women that she knew. When women always asked her where all the men in the club are, she didn't even have an answer to that question herself. Now here she was listening to a young, uneducated woman, obviously from a totally different walk of life, answer all of her problems. Morgan looked around the club and thought about the money that she was making and wasn't making. She needed a partner from that other side of the fence; a partner that could turn a nice bar into a club where people from all walks of life could have a great time. She wanted dick for her single and well to do female friends and colleagues, and this young woman, even with her inexperience to the actual business, had the ability to provide it. Without hesitation, Morgan looked up and said, "Sister Sister, I would like to make you my partner. Now come on over here with me so that you can meet our auntie and boss."

CHAPTER TWENTY-TWO

"BREAKING BREAD TOGETHER"

"Morgan this is Cantrell..." Ameesha said while smiling, "and by now you and Sylvia don't need an introduction."

Morgan thought to herself about how much money Sylvia had made for the club with her influx of new patrons. Business had been booming three nights a week for a month straight now since Sylvia signed on. "Yes Sylvia is my golden Child, I would kill over her!" All of the ladies burst out laughing. "Sylvia and Ameesha, this is my better half Darius Thompson. He gets on my damn nerves at times but I'm not ready to dump him just yet." Laughter filled the room! Even from a few patrons who overheard the statement.

Cantrell leaned over to Darius and whispered, "I see that this is going to be one of those mornings." Darius gave him a quick look of agreement and both men smiled at one another.

The loud speaker went off: "Morgan party of five your table is ready, Morgan party of five your table is ready." Everyone hurried to their seats. Melvin's pancakes were to die for and everyone present was in a hurry to see the afterlife.

"Oh my! That was delicious!" Morgan said in her fat girl voice and everyone nodded their heads in agreement. "So Mr. Solomon, Ameesha tells me that she met my girl wonder Sylvia through you... where did you find this diamond?"

Sylvia and Cantrell shot one another a nervous glance, but Cantrell was quick on his toes. "My uncle used to work on her aunt's vehicles. I've known Sylvia since she was a kid." Sylvia gave Cantrell a big Kool aid smile.

"Well let me thank you for the informal invite because this little lady here has been the scratch to my itch." Morgan said.

Cantrell smiled at Morgan and said, "The way I see it, your network determines your net worth. He or she who limits their connections, ultimately makes their world smaller as well as their bank account."

Morgan couldn't do anything but agree. "So Ameesha, Sylvia and I were thinking, we want you to be our partner in a win win deal; we are going to bring Myron Kincaid, the guy who made that song *Love, Lust, and Leisure* to the club and it's going to be a huge success! Now before you say anything, let me say this, I know that you have been to club concerts featuring R&B acts before and they were a bust. But Sylvia came up with an idea to do Sigma Gamma Rho's annual charity female auction the same night. She is inviting all of the hood guys to come out and blow wads of cash on the women in the auction. We are going to raise money for a good cause, while raising the roof in the club! We can't lose! All that we need from you is ten grand, we will both put up ten grand a piece as well. You can even work the door, that way you will recoup your $10k before either of us see a return."

Ameesha thought to herself, did she really want to risk ten grand doing something that wasn't even in her field? She felt a kick from under the table, it was Cantrell. He gave her a harsh look that said "Say yes dammit."

"Uhmm ummm uhhhhh yes, uhh yes I would like to partner with you two lovely ladies..." Ameesha said nervously.

"Yaayyyyyy!" Morgan and Sylvia started to cheer, then Sylvia said, "We will have a contract drawn up for you by tomorrow and we will need the funds in a cashier's check made out to Trinity Fire Ent."

That surprised the hell out of Ameesha coming from Sylvia; her little ruffian buddy sounded so professional now! "Dang Shaquesha, you don't have to put the pressure on me like that geesh!" Everyone at the table burst out laughing.

Morgan chimed in, "Oh and so that the guys don't feel left out - Darius didn't I overhear you saying that you needed more trucks to haul off all of the old black top from that big repair job on the Norwood lateral?"

"Yes babe, you did hear that. Not being able to remove the debris fast enough has us behind schedule big time." Darius explained.

Morgan continued, "Well Ameesha tells me that Mr.

Cantrell has two large dump trucks and is looking to invest in another."

Cantrell was about to speak but he felt a kick from under the table. It was Ameesha giving him the *Negro I got this, and buy another truck* look.

"Is this true? Oh my God, I can make you some serious money my brother! Here, take my card and meet me at my office Monday morning at 8am with pictures of your trucks, as well as background info on your drivers."

Cantrell stuttered, "uhhh uhhhh noooo problem my brother. I will see you Monday at 8."

Darius threw his card out on the table to pay for breakfast and said, "With all of you vultures here trying to make a dollar, I'm going to be the only person writing off this business/ breakfast meeting."

Cantrell laughed! He could definitely appreciate that business move.

CHAPTER TWENTY-THREE

"THE TRINITY"

Club Fire was packed! Morgan, Sylvia and Ameesha all decided to wear red for the event to symbolize their little female trinity of three flames. Three bad chicks, all bad in different ways respectively. Morgan often pondered her new friendships and realized how powerful people, especially African American women, could be when they worked together. In a time where the norm was black women arguing and fighting one another, she had managed to link up with Sylvia, a street chick, that she had met through her childhood friend Ameesha, who eventually helped turn her mediocre bar into a cash cow club. For a year straight now Club Fire had been going strong three nights per week! They had Buy You a Drink Monday's where all of the ballers came in and basically bought out the bar just so the ladies could drink free all night. Women were coming from as far as Chicago to be splurged on and catered to for the night at Club Fire. They had karaoke on Wednesdays, thanks to Sylvia, it had become a great mixture of corporate as well as hood people who all had one thing in common: the love for a stiff drink, music, and a good laugh. Then there was Saturday's, their total pandemonium night! They started bringing B List R&B acts like Thomas Shumpert, Christine Pennington, and Abigail the Songstress. The smooth R&B artist made for a very chill and upscale atmosphere for people from all walks of life. Saturday's brought out the corporate dudes that enjoyed the more inviting nature of the street women, and the street dudes that loved the challenge of the corporate women.

The club's revenue was up 1000% and Ameesha was in the process of starting the ladies a real estate investing firm so they could use the construction savvy of Morgan's boyfriend Darius. Her boyfriend Cantrell had a direct connection to affordable and hungry labor from down in the projects that could aid them in doing some high end remodels, earning them some extra cash on the side. Tonight they had Lava Jones in the building, along with the rest of the female cast from the hit show *My Sisters Keeper.* The local men were bound to go bananas over the hot bodied and classy women who were set to grace the stage with Lava. Morgan emerged from her thoughts and observed Sylvia in her hot red business pants suit that fit her like a glove. She had a knack for showing a hoochie amount of ass, without being half naked. Sylvia was at the bar motioning to the runners to get more champagne into the coolers behind the bar. She eyed Ameesha, whose body looked unbelievably sexy in her red dress that was open in the back all the way down to the crack of her ample backside. She had the male bartenders watching her every move. Tonight was their big night, they were doing the after party for the Cincinnati Music Festival, and if things went as planned, they would all be counting major loot.

Things picked up so much at the club that Morgan hired Ameesha on as her bar manager. The influx of patrons deemed to be too much for her aunt to handle. When she offered her aunt a new office and a paperwork position, she jumped for joy. Morgan heard her phone chime; she had received a text from a member of her street team letting her know that the concert had just let out. She walked the room letting everyone know to assume their positions. With 500 in pre-sale tickets sold, they were about to see a rush like they had never seen before.

Ameesha surveyed the room, it was 1am and every booth in the club was full. Ballers from Chicago to Louisville were swimming in bottles and women in their respective booths. The guys from Sylvia's hood aka Down the Way were acting a fool. They had women holding bottles of champagne in their hands as if they were mixed drinks. Hanson Thomas of the Cincinnati Bengals had a booth full of groupies showing love to him and his entourage. There were two separate groups of women balling out. Ameesha knew one of them because she owned some sort of eyebrow shop or beauty bar in midtown. The other one looked to be a street chick. Maybe she was the girlfriend of a hustler because she was completely iced out along with her crew and everyone seemed to pay homage to them. Ameesha assumed the rest of the booths to be full of out of towners. She didn't see any familiar faces except for Morgan's brother Prez and his gang of lunatics, but it wasn't as if she knew a bunch of people anyways.

"Omg we did it!" Sylvia screamed, just as the smash hit *We Made it* blasted through the speakers. "There is at least

$200,000 in the back room with auntie, and that's not counting the pre-sale ticket money or the monies from the bar! We even raised $80,000 for the sorority! My homeboy Tocca that owns the barbershop on Beekman St. near Millville bid $20,000 for two of the women of Sigma Gamma Rho sorority. "

Morgan and Ameesha weren't shocked at all. Cantrell and Darius were literally counting people, so they had given Morgan the thumbs up 2 hours before the party even ended. Morgan clearly seen the wads of cash in the hands of the men who were trying to bid on the ladies in the auction. The men were already popping bottles and celebrating the success of their ladies. Sylvia wished that Bleed could be there, but she understood that his name and presence was bad for business. No man in Cincinnati would feel comfortable balling out while Trevor Bledsoe's scheming and murdering ass was in the building. Sylvia laughed because most women would let times like this cause them to question their relationship, but not her, she knew exactly who she had signed up to love and if they had to celebrate in private, so be it.

Ameesha said, "This is only the beginning ladies! Now it is time for me to put my part of the plan into motion! She never gave up on executing *Lonzo's plan*. Now, with her new networking connections, she could do so with ease. Next year, we will be celebrating the success of our next big ventures in Ibiza Spain. I heard that it is beautiful there!"

CHAPTER TWENTY-FOUR

"LOOSE LIPS SINK SHIPS"

Sylvia sat in the hairdresser listening to the typical basic bitch gossip; there was a long drawn out discussion about everything big, who had the biggest house, biggest bankroll, biggest dick etc. Sylvia hated basic bitches; the types of chicks that couldn't see past looking good and spending some niggas money. She often wondered why the best hairdressers were always at the hood shops, and what the conversations were like in the shops in Hyde Park and Kenwood. She answered her own question when she realized that Morgan hung with white privileged girls, and she said those white hoes were the most ratchet. Ameesha was super square, but even though her way of saying things was proper the bitch was still ratchet. The hairdresser can be informative too though. Chicks gossip so much they end up telling all of their men's business. Sylvia once overheard a chick in the hairdresser saying that her dude put 20 bands on Bleed's head. Sylvia listened some more first to make sure that the threat was real, and when she heard the name Flip, she knew it was real. Flip was getting real money up in Price Hill, and even though he was a bitch nigga, he kept a gang of shooters on retainer. Before getting under the dryer, Sylvia went to the bathroom, called Bleed, and told him what she had just heard. Bleed asked her to describe the girl and to describe what she was wearing. Sylvia gave him a detailed description of the chick and Bleed had his goons snatch her when she left the hairdresser. Word on the streets was that Flip paid $200k to get her back, and agreed to squash the beef because his girl had been scared into telling all of his spots. With nowhere to hide, he wasn't in a position to go at it with Bleed. Sylvia couldn't believe that even after that incident, bitches still ran off at the mouth around women they didn't know. It was one hoe in particular today that was irking her damn nerves and she was this middle aged chick named Layla. Layla was sitting there bragging about all of the men that had cashed out on her. She was blasting out the guys that she had tricked and stolen from. This chick had to be 35+, and was bragging about using up 22-year-old boys still to this day. She could tell that Layla was one of those chicks that used to be bad, but now life and too many different dicks in her mouth had worn her down. She still had the framework of a younger woman but was a little pudgy around the waist. Most elder dudes would be happy to have her though. Her face looked, worn, stressed, and just plain tired, yet she still wasn't unattractive. She was one of those high yellow chicks that had white woman wrinkles on her face. She wore a red LV purse; it was hot, but you could tell that she sucked a dick for it over ten years ago. The only thing up to date on the chick was her damn shoes and they were the new red bottoms that Kim Michaels wore in the video for her new song *Spoil Me*. Sylvia hated old, unpolished chicks. She concluded that the bitch must have had a 20-year-old daughter or something who fucked some young baller for those shoes, and Layla was just wearing them. It shocked Sylvia to hear that Layla was the one who put those Detroit killers on Lil Cody from McMicken St. a few years back. She was talking about the shit as if his murder had been solved and his killers had been put away for life already. The truth was that they never found Cody; they found his apartment ransacked and it looked as if there had been a struggle. Word on the street was that a lot of drugs and money had been taken but the authorities never found a body. Sylvia thought to herself, "*This is exactly why I hate loose dick niggas! They do all of that low-key shit: switching up cars, cell phones, wearing work uniforms to disguise their movements etc., yet they will stick their dicks in a gossiping ass hoe like this big mouth bitch Layla. Bitches like her will get an entire neighborhood indicted.*" Sylvia started reading a magazine to calm herself down when she heard Layla mention Morgan's dude Darius. Morgan had told her that her and dude bumped heads initially because he assumed that she was a sack chaser. When they finally did link up, he apologized and explained that a woman had done him really bad when he was younger. She fucked him up emotionally and it was rumored that she got him for fifty grand without ever giving him any pussy. Sylvia continued to look at the magazine but she was all ears to what Layla was saying.

"Yeah bitch, I crack those legit niggas too! They are a little harder because they have accountants and shit; they don't just have an open bag like street niggas do. I had to really play the damsel in distress role on this guy that I met up at UC named Darius. After that shit with Lil Cody, my name was mud in the streets, so I got me a little apartment up in Clifton and started taking some classes at UC. Those little college boys didn't know what hit them. I got in good with the school girls and they told me which dudes were the ones from rich families, and believe it or not, there were a lot of guys with money on campus. See, on campus you will meet a guy that is already rich from running his family's business, and he simply wants to go back to school to learn to do something different. Well I came across this guy named Darius. Word around campus was that he had started a couple of clothing lines his sophomore year and they did really well. Then I found out that he owned that high end line called Waldorf Conceptions. I tricked him into getting at me at a concert, and upon meeting him, I saw that he was open for games that even the dumbest of hood dudes wouldn't go for. I worked him good, from the "Tracy stole my rent money" hustle, to the "Sick relative that needs money" trick. I had him eating out the palm of my hand and didn't even give him any pussy. I had to get at least 40 or 50 thousand up out of him. When he did press the issue of sex, I let him eat this pussy, and then acted like my stomach hurt." Layla told the story as if it were a game and the women in the hairdresser burst out laughing. It was hard to believe that anyone could be so stupid, but Sylvia thought otherwise. Men and women, both, who were from that legitimate world had been robbing clueless hustlers via deeds and contracts since the beginning of time. It wasn't unfathomable that a street chick could work a square if she drug him out of his office and into the street. Sylvia was out from under the dryer and getting the finishing touches on her new hair-do. The bitch Layla was still running off at the mouth, and it irked Sylvia's nerves because it was Morgan's dude that she was clowning. She decided to shoot Morgan a text:

Sylvia: Hey sister... I'm sitting in the shop trying to get beautified and guess who is sitting here running off at the mouth?

Morgan: Who sis?

Sylvia: That the bitch who hurt Darius back in the day! She is in here talking real reckless about him too. You should come up here and slap this hoe.

Morgan: As much as I would lovvvve to do so, I have a lot to lose if I get charged with a crime. In the business world, stuff like that will end your career.

Sylvia: Yea, I get it. Well hell, give me permission to slap this bitch.

Morgan: LOL you are grown, I can't stop you from burning a bitch face with a curling iron and slapping her out of the stylist chair.

Sylvia: You are a sick bitch LOL

Sylvia liked Morgan's idea though... Although she was a square, her brother and his friends' bullshit had rubbed off on her. Sylvia figured that she would follow Morgan's instructions to the tee. After paying her stylist, she eyed a pair of hot irons on the counter. She played it off as if she was looking in the mirror, slid the irons off the counter, and walked towards an unsuspecting Layla. With the quickness she pressed the hot irons on Layla's face! The bitch squealed like a stuck pig and her legs started kicking wildly. When she tried to get up, Sylvia dropped the iron and pushed her back down. Everyone in the shop were frightened with disbelief. Sylvia started punching Layla as hard and fast as she could, and screaming, "Darius is like a brother to me bitch! You have had this ass whipping coming for over a decade now! Be lucky that I didn't kill you bitch, you old scandalous hoe!" She grabbed a heavy pair of hair trimmers and cracked Layla a few more times with them while yelling, "And this is for Cody bitch! You set up a real nigga." Sylvia ran up out of the shop before anyone had a chance to call the police.

CHAPTER TWENTY-FIVE

"WISE WORDS"

Cantrell walked into Maarku's Quickie Mart/Gas station. " As-Salaam-Alaikum my brother," greeted Maarku.

" Wa-Alaikum-Salaam," Cantrell replied to Maarku's Afro-Arab greeting of welcome and peace.

"I haven't seen you in a while brother Solomon. New girl, new business, what has been keeping you away?" Maarku asked.

"Life is good brother... I met a woman who has come along and turned my life upside down, in a good way. She has shined a light of goodness upon me that I have never been touched by before. She brought a sense of peace into my life that I've experienced with no other woman. She even used some of her own connections and started me a construction debris removal company." Cantrell replied with honor.

"That sounds like the work of Allah brother. Only Allah gives us what we need, even when we aren't sure of what we need." Maarku expressed.

Cantrell shook his head in acknowledgement of Maarku's words.

"What's been going on with you though? How have you been over these past few months?" Cantrell asked.

"Me, I went to Nigeria for a month to see my wife and children. To my surprise, my fourteen-year-old son had learned to play the violin. He put on a full concert for me when I arrived at my home and it was good. My oldest daughter, who is twenty, joined a dance ensemble in London. My wife says that she is very good as well. She actually makes $200,000 US dollars to dance for this company, so I guess she has to be very good to earn that." Maarku chuckled. "She demands that I come to see here dance in Austria at the end of next month. You and your new woman should accompany me and my wife."

Cantrell thought about going to Europe with Ameesha. She would love to do something like that with him, and he felt the same way. "I may have to take you up on that big bro. She just helped me get a passport too, so this trip must have been already written." Said Cantrell.

Maarku shook his head and said, "Praise Allah brother. She has seemingly sharpened your sword to perfection. I need a woman like that here in America. I mean, my sisters do a good job running the gas station, yet they still require too much of my time and energy. I really would love to branch off into other business ventures but I can't count on them as much as I would like. I came across a very high end boutique while I was in Ghana. Although they sold

African clothing, I think that Americans would find the items very stylish. I want to put one here in your Kenwood Mall and see how it does."

Cantrell instantly thought of Morgan. She would be great at organizing, executing, and running something like that. He figured if they went on the trip next month, he would make sure to plug his woman. Cantrell spoke with enthusiasm, "I read all of the books that you gave me. I really liked that last one titled *Servants of Allah*, it gave me a whole different perspective on how I should be living my life today based on the traditions and beliefs of our ancestors."

"Wisdom is all over you brother Cantrell. A year from now, you will really be walking in the light of your ancestors and doing Allah's will. This American system is not for you, not for us. A lot of times African Americans ask me how is it that the native Africans and Arabs get to come over here and own gas stations, prime real estate, and other businesses. My answer to that is unity. Unity is the key to success for any nation of people. When I first came to America some years ago, I recognized how profitable selling bootleg CD's and DVD's was. Most Americans haven't realized that the cd stand has phased out the big record stores. You can't find a record store anywhere nowadays, but have you ever asked yourself where did that money go? Well, the answer is, it went to the cd stands! Then there is hair: hair for braiding and hair for weaving. When I recognized that American women were paying top dollar for hair, I put my feelers out to my African brothers in India as well as China. Within weeks, I had access to hair for wholesale prices and instead of allowing Americans to not buy from me simply because they believe that Africans sell fake or cheap stuff, I found me a beautiful American woman to partner with, and allowed her to be the face of that venture. Not many Africans here have cars, so I took the money that I made and invested in a car dealership. Now every African in Cincinnati buys their cars from me. I even sell the cabs to the African owned cab companies. Finally, I opened my gas station. All of the Africans, including the cab companies, get gas from me in the morning. They get up early and wait in line to fill up, just so they won't have to support the businesses of some other race or group of people. I rent property to all of the Africans in the area and I support other African businesses as well. I only eat at African restaurants; I only buy clothing from African boutiques; and only African tradesman can work on my properties. I only use African mechanics for my cars and all of this keeps the African dollar with the Africans, while we pull money from the Americans. We Africans also stick within our communities. We eat, live, and party together, therefore we have no use for the expensive clothing that you African Americans feel that you need to wear to impress the world. That's the blessing of a community my brother. There is no one to impress, everyone is rooting for one another to win. My brother, create your own world and live in it. Start with your family and never venture too far outside of your family structure. Invest money into your family and your circle, and life will balance itself out for you. Treat your women with kindness and sincerity because they are the closest thing to you, and most importantly, live for your children."

Cantrell took it all in, and once again Maarku was right. Too many times men, especially black men, got caught up living for everyone but their families. A man's woman and children are impressed by his presence, not his presents.

"Sorry that I can't chat longer with you today. My wife is arriving today and I must pick her up from the airport up near Dayton. If you can stop by early next week, I will have more books for you as well as some items and products for your women that my wife has brought with her from our country." Maarku said, interrupting Trell's thoughts.

"I will most definitely do that. And please, if your wife can cook thiebou djenne, could you have her prepare some for me, my girl, and my partner? The woman that you hooked me up with only cooks on the weekends and my friend Flee wants to eat it every day. It's to the point now that I charge him double just to go and get him a plate. He goes crazy over the cabbage and carrots."

Maarku burst into laughter, "Here give your friend this card. She cooks daily, and if he gave her money upfront she would prepare as much for him as he would like. It is wrong of you to charge a friend extra to eat. That is a crime punishable by beheading in my country!" Maarku burst into laughter again. "Peace my brother Cantrell, and let's pray that Allah gives your partner a full belly hahahahaha."

CHAPTER TWENTY-SIX

"LOOK OUT PARADISE, HERE COMES TROUBLE!"

Cantrell was lying in bed next to Ameesha, looking down at her, wondering how such an innocent looking women could be so nasty. The woman didn't want him to go outside earlier, but he told her that he had things to do. She insisted on giving him a blow job before he left out, and that was at around 11am. Now it was 11pm, and 100 blowjobs later, he was still in the house. She got like that sometimes when she was on her cycle; she just wanted to suck him dry all fucking day. It dawned on him that he shouldn't be complaining though because a woman like that would be considered a blessing to other men. He was about to rub his dick on her face to see if she would suck it again when he heard his phone vibrating. He reached over to grab it, and the name that came across the screen made his heart drop to the floor: *Lil Trevor.* It irked Cantrell to have to answer the phone, but it was the Lil homie, so what was a man to do?

"Bleed my nigga, what it do?" Cantrell said in the best happy voice that he could muster.

"Same ole same ole OG. I'm kind of in a pinch though and need a favor from someone that I can trust." Bleed hinted.

"What do you need Lil homie, shoot?" Trell asked.

Bleed explained, "Man I've been working too hard family, it's time for me to take a nap. My problem is that my girl put me out, and I got all of my prize possessions in my van. I need you to drive my van to wherever you see fit that is safe and hold it down until I get some rest. I will be back to get it when I get my mind right and find a new place."

Cantrell figured that was easy enough. He knew that Trevor wouldn't have any guns or drugs in a van that he wanted him to drive and at best, it was money and jewelry. Cantrell told him to meet him at the big store on Ridge. He would park his car there and then ride with him to get the van.

***

Cantrell had known Lil Trevor aka Bleed for years. Trevor was the down ass young boy on the block back in the day when he would try to sneak and hustle up on 13th street. He used to give Trevor the pack to run out to the junkies' cars while he sat in the house without anyone knowing he was hustling up there. He gave Bleed a percentage, and Bleed loved him for the opportunity to get some money. It worked really well for a while, but just like all young boys, Trevor got too ambitious. He decided to get his own pack and steal

Cantrell's licks, but unfortunately for him, one of the junkies had turned informant. Trevor got caught and carted off to the juvenile detention center. He just knew that he was going to DYS but when he got to court, he saw his mom and Trell. Trell had gotten him a lawyer, and the lawyer made it seem as if some unknown dealer forced Trevor to sell his drugs. He painted a picture that Trevor was just an innocent kid from a tough neighborhood. The lawyer said that the bad neighborhood and society were more to blame than young Trevor, and the judge ate it up. He sentenced him to one year probation, and said that he had to stay in school and keep his grades up or he would be getting sent up state. Lil Trevor paged Cantrell as soon as he was released, apologizing for crossing him. He promised that he would never do it again. Trell told him that the block up there was hot anyways and that he would be doing his thing in his own hood for a while. Trevor was pissed, but he understood. Cantrell always kept his ear to the street, monitoring what young Trevor was doing. He heard that all of the little guys up there were calling him a snitch for not going to DYS for a direct sell. They said one little guy in particular by the name of Deuce picked a fight with Trevor over the snitching allegations. Back then, snitching was a definite no no in the hood. How most folks told the story, the much bigger kid Deuce caught Trevor with two good punches and dropped him, but to Deuce's surprise, Trevor had a little 22 caliber revolver on him and gave the kid two to the leg.

From that point on, Cantrell heard nothing but bad things about little Trevor: robberies, shootings, and extortion. Funny thing was that whenever he would see Trevor, he would still act like the little appreciative kid from 10 years prior. He had grown to be a goon and would always say to Trell if he needed someone hit, he would do them in for free because he owed him one. Cantrell was used to handling his own beefs though. He had been busting his gun since age 12, but this one particular time, a couple of guys jumped Cantrell in the club while he was solo with his ice on. He was stunting in a club out on the Westside, trying to chase this little thick chick named Netta. He didn't realize that his reputation in his own hood didn't travel with him to that side of town. The next morning, he had text after text after text from Trevor asking if he was ok because he had heard what happened. Cantrell tried calling his phone to see what he heard, or if anyone said who the dudes were that did it, but Trevor wasn't answering. Cantrell started making calls trying to put together his own investigation into the matter when a text came through from Trevor that said: Lil Julie that I used to mess with back in the day got your ice big homie. She lives at 713 Race St, call her, the number is 513-555-7831.

Cantrell knew not to ask any further questions. He gave the girl a call and rode down to Race St. to get his jewels. The young girl came out and handed him a black gym bag. He opened it and almost puked when he looked inside. His ice was literally covered in blood! He closed the bag instantly and rode to an elderly woman's house that he used as a stash spot to clean off the jewels and to burn the gym bag. After that, him and Trevor's relationship was a favor for a favor. Trevor would sometimes hit a lick for a lot of work and would dump it right on Cantrell for a super cheap price. In turn, he might have an open beef with someone that he couldn't handle publicly because the cops would know that he did it. He would call on Cantrell to get it handled for him and he always did.

***

Today was different. There was no serious beef, just a simple lift to get a van. When he hopped in with Trevor, Trevor didn't say much of anything. That was fine with Cantrell because he was still exhausted from getting blowed all day by Ameesha. He just let his seat back and dozed off.

Cantrell hadn't been sleep that long when he heard a hard tap on his window. He and Trevor had been pulled over. The cops wanted to search the car and were acting rather hostile. Trevor turned to him and whispered, "Damn OG, I just realized that three bangers are under your seat. I would claim them but you know just like I do that they will just take my statement, allow me to take the case for two of them, and still stick you with the one. We will have to just let them take us down and I will take the case at the indictment hearing." Cantrell gave him the ok nod and they both allowed the cops to do their jobs without giving them any hassle.

CHAPTER TWENTY-SEVEN

"BACK AGAINST THE WALL"

"Bledsoe you have a visit." The officer yelled while tapping on his cell door with a flashlight.

Bleed knew what this was. Visiting hours had been over with, this had to be the FBI coming to squeeze him about his record and threatening to take the gun charges federal. This was the walk that most street guys feared. This was when you knew that no matter how much money you had, it would not save you. Bleed didn't really think about the feds, even with getting caught red handed with those guns. He knew that his prints weren't on any of them because he didn't place them there. His young shooter Bodies put those guns in the car over a month ago and parked the whip in this old lady named Ms. Agnus driveway. He feared that the cops had placed bugs and a tracking device on his Maxima, so he decided to park it and get a ride to Ms. Agnus house to grab the slider. He completely forgot that the guns were under the passenger's seat. They were supposed to get rid of the weapons, but the cops got on them too fast after the murder, and they never had a chance to take them to their spot down on the river and toss them in. Ever since his shooter Ishmael was found guilty of murder because the cameras on the bridge caught him pulling over and throwing guns into the water, they always took their throwaways all the way down to the fishing areas on the river near the casinos.

Bleed was ushered into a room full of detectives. The room only contained a table, a chair, and an extremely bright light that made his eyes hurt. The officer shoved him down into the chair and when he looked up, he saw a very familiar face. "Trevor fucking Bledsoe," Detective Stanton said while tapping on the table. "Looks like you have gotten yourself into some doggy poop. How did a smart criminal like yourself get caught red-handed with guns? Better yet, murder weapons?"

Bleed shot the detective a blank stare.

Detective Stanton continued, "When I heard this, I said to myself that someone had set my buddy up. I've had him hook lined and sinker on several homicides, but he has always managed to slip through the cracks. Whatever or whoever caused you to have this mental fart, you have to tell me about them, because guys like you don't slip."

Bleed wanted to tell him so bad that this was just a goofy mistake, but he figured goofy and homicide didn't go in the same sentence.

"Mr. Bledsoe, this is my friend agent Avery from the Bureau of Alcohol, Firearms and Tobacco. This is his friend

Mrs. Jennifer Dean-Wales from the Drug Enforcement Agency, and this is her friend Bob Schultz from the Federal Bureau of Investigations. We have a few more agencies lined up to take a bite out of your black ass, do you get the picture asshole?" Detective Stanton asked. "Everyone, can you please step out of the room and allow me some time with Mr. Bledsoe please?" The detective continued.

Everyone left the interrogation room one by one.

Detective Stanton went on, "Funny thing is, I'm going to bat for you on this one because I'm not a dirty cop. I know those aren't your guns, and I know that you haven't killed anyone. I'm not going to lie to you; I really enjoy locking black guys up and I'm not even a racist. I enjoy locking black guys up because a lot of you are too stupid to be free. You commit crimes out of boredom, you get online and post pictures of drugs, guns, and money; throw up gang signs, and do all sorts of other things to incriminate yourselves. Now if a guy wants to throw his life away for being stupid, that's fine with me, but those silly cases don't require good detective work. Any pencil pusher or screen watcher can catch those idiots. Me, I like to crack real cases. I like to track down and lock up the real slicksters like yourself. I just can't allow myself to beat you, knowing that you didn't make this mistake or bad move, someone else did this. I'm going to put a pawn on the table for you my friend. My FBI friend Mr. Schultz has an old open murder that he believes your buddy Mr. Solomon was the shooter on. Some shit about an Arab running around selling kilos of heroine behind his pops back who owned a corner store down on Linn St. Somehow the kid gets found dead in the dumpster; the kilos were missing, and the streets were screaming that some thirteen-year-old shooter named Boobie aka Cantrell Solomon did it. Detectives brought him in back then, but someone put some serious bread behind the kid because Jew lawyers showed up so fast that no one could ever get the kid's story. Since it was only hearsay and there was no real evidence, the case went cold. The father has been lobbying for the government to investigate the case as a hate crime. He wants the heroine accusations ignored, and he says he believes that his son was murdered by blacks who hated Arabs for doing business in their communities. Over twenty years later, he is still screaming for justice. I want you to take a second look at those papers. First one is from the ATF. It outlines how long they will give you for the types of weapons that you were caught with, which is no less than 30 years. No lawyer can save you from that." Bleed read over the papers and the detective was right. It seemed as if the guns would basically give him the death penalty if convicted. "Now that second one is from the DEA. Read it and weep." Detective Stanton instructed. Bleed read the second set of paperwork. It was an affidavit from some kid in prison saying that Bleed sold him an ounce of crack. Funny thing is, Bleed remembered giving the kid the ounce for free to get on his feet but the fool posted it online with a caption that said, "About to get this money." Needless to say, he got bagged long before he got any money. Now he was willing to testify and say that Bleed gave it to him.

The DEA made a clear outline of how they would use the kid's testimony to pitch to a prosecutor that Bleed was part of a murderous, drug trafficking gang. With his record and street name, he wouldn't stand a chance in federal court.

"There are a lot more angles to attack you from Mr. Bledsoe, including state charges. I'm willing to tell everyone to leave; every agent and every detective, and I will personally discredit every informant. All I ask of you is to give your friend Mr. Solomon over to my buddy Mr. Schultz. If I can do him this favor, it will help me climb up the ladders of law enforcement. Oh, I forgot to mention your queen, Ms. Sylvia Wright aka Syl. Trust and believe that I will let the feds nail her to the fucking cross if you opt to not continue to play our little game. Sacrifice the pawn, keep your queen, go free, and let's get back to playing chess." The detective offered.

Detective Stanton walked out and left Bleed there to ponder his options. He thought to himself how he couldn't let them take Sylvia down; she didn't deserve it. Bleed had known Cantrell ever since he was a kid, and although they had taken different paths, anytime he had called on Trell he was there for him. Whether it be for bond money, help with a beef, or even for an apartment or house to hide out in, he could always count on his big homie Trell. He couldn't sink Trell, but damn he couldn't stand by and watch Syl sink either.

CHAPTER TWENTY-EIGHT

"WHY ME? WHY US!"

Ameesha was sound asleep when the phone rang. She rolled over to realize that Cantrell was gone and it was 5:30am. She picked up Cantrell's house phone to hear, "You have a collect call from the County Detainment Center." She thought that she had to be dreaming, but she hit the button anyways.

"Meesha, Meesha are you there?" Trell screamed.

"Cantrell is that you?" Ameesha said in an extremely frazzled voice.

"Yes baby it's me, the craziest thing just happened. I left out of the house to help a friend move some things out his girl's house because they were having issues, in the process of doing that, we got pulled over and he had guns on him. I don't know if it's because he didn't have any permits for the guns or if they are stolen but they are holding me and him until we go to court at 9am. I don't even know what I'm being charged with. What I need for you to do is call my attorney, Tom Goldstein, and have him to meet you down at courtroom A at the detention center at 9am. Can you do that for me please?" Cantrell pleaded.

"You have 60 seconds left for this call," the operator interrupted.

"Cantrell what is going on? Who were you with? Why did you leave out of the house at that time of night?" Ameesha rambled.

"Baby, just do what I said please!" Cantrell screamed.

The line went dead.

Court was total chaos. Ameesha had never been in trouble before. She never even had a parking ticket, so sitting in a room full of Cincinnati's rowdiest, loudest, and uncivilized people didn't sit well with her at all. She only got to get a glimpse of Cantrell, his lawyer met him at the podium in front of the judge. A few words were exchanged and then he rushed him back through the side door from which he came. His attorney alerted her that he was being charged with weapons under disability, normally something that the judge would give a fairly low bond on, but for some unforeseen reason the prosecution requested no bond and the judge agreed to it. He said that he wouldn't know what was really going on until the next court date which was set for 2 weeks from today. He gave her a note from Cantrell that had a location on it and the code to a safe. He wanted her to give the attorney $10,000. She thought, no one pays $10,000 to an attorney for a simple mistake. Something was going on and she was terrified. Also on the note, he asked that she not mention him being locked up to anyone because it would affect how people viewed him. He wouldn't want Darius to believe that his new contractor was a criminal, and he wouldn't want Morgan to think that some type of drama with him could interfere or hurt all of the good things that had been going on for the ladies at the club. So for the time being, he wanted her to say that he was out of town dealing with a family tragedy.

CHAPTER TWENTY-NINE

"OUR SISTERS KEEPER"

It troubled Morgan and Sylvia that Ameesha took a leave of absence to deal with personal issues, yet she didn't disclose the issues. They both felt that they all had become close enough friends that she could come to them about anything, but maybe they were wrong? Morgan figured that it had to be something going on with Ameesha's boyfriend Cantrell because Darius said he now mails his checks from the trucking contracts to a post office box, when normally Cantrell would stop by his office and chat a bit when it was time to collect his checks. He was also worried because he hadn't actually talked to Cantrell in several months. He didn't even know if he had ever made it back in town from dealing with his family issues. Something strange was definitely going on, Sylvia thought to herself. Bleed disappeared around the same time that Cantrell did. She had checked the Clerk of Courts site for Bleed's name, and they had no one in custody by that name. She would have looked up Cantrell, but she never knew his last name. To be honest, she wasn't even sure if Cantrell was really his first name. For some strange reason she believed that this all had some connection to when Renzo got killed. It was her womanly intuition that was nudging her towards the Renzo angle. Maybe Cantrell and Bleed just so happened to be together when someone who was seeking revenge for Renzo's death snatched them both up. Maybe they were both dead in some abandoned building, or dead in the back of an old parking lot. She didn't feel that her connection to him was broken though, so in some weird way she felt that her lover was still alive. She was going to ask Rae Lynn if she had heard anything on her end, but after seeing how Rae Lynn blew her off at Renzo's funeral, she decided to just let the little stuck up bitch grieve. She knew what she had to do. She had to find out where Ameesha was staying, because it was obvious that she was hiding something or hiding from something.

CHAPTER THIRTY

"CRY ME A RIVER"

Ameesha couldn't believe it... her worst fears had come to pass, building a life with an ex-street guy and having it all come crumbling down with him going to prison. Cantrell had promised her that he left the streets alone. He promised that he would always be there for her, and now she was sitting there, two months pregnant with his baby and waiting to see him in the detention center. She knew what she had to do though. If he still wanted to flirt with the street life, she would take her baby and move far away from the city. If he managed to go to prison on these charges, he would never see her and her baby again.

Cantrell wondered what was going on in Ameesha's mind. He knew that she must be scared to death, not only for him, but for herself and the baby. As he stood in line waiting to approach the visiting booth, he could see Ameesha sitting there looking stressed. She had a look of uncertainty on her face that he had never seen before, yet he understood why she looked that way. He gathered himself as well as his words as they called his name and motioned for him to approach the booth. He leaned in to kiss the glass as if he were kissing her, but she pulled back and started going off. He didn't understand a single word of her rant, but he felt her pain. He wanted to grab her and hold her close, but he couldn't. He spoke softly, "Baby I didn't do anything, anything at all. Don't convict me of this when even the court system hasn't convicted me yet. This is all on Bleed; he is a stand-up dude, and he knows that he has to clear my name. Unfortunately for me, you, and the baby, it will be a process."

Ameesha stared at him. He looked so vulnerable and defeated. Even though she was angry, she couldn't find it in her heart to kick him when he was down. Ameesha calmed herself and spoke, "If you truly had nothing to do with this, why won't they let you go?"

"Baby I done some things when I was younger… Things that I don't even like to speak on anymore. I try to forget those things, move on with life, and do better for myself but unfortunately law enforcement never forgets. They will hold me and try to scare me about some old unsolved cases. They blew the weapons under disability thing way out of proportion, all in an attempt to squeeze me for information or scare me into a plea. I will do neither; I will not talk, nor will I plea. The only way that I will go to prison for this is if Bleed puts me into whatever they got him for. If he were to put me in it, he still would have to take the stand and testify against me, and I seriously doubt that he would do that. I will fight this case to the end, until my last breath." Cantrell explained. He did not want to be there anymore that she wanted him to be.

"Do you think that this Bleed character could possibly try to sink you to save himself?" Ameesha asked with a look of concern.

"No way… although I don't run with him, I know the caliber of dude that he is. It isn't in him to snitch." Cantrell stated confidently.

The phone went dead; their 15 minutes were up. Ameesha watched as the love of her life was escorted back to whatever hell hole that they were keeping him in.

CHAPTER THIRTY-ONE

"LIFE WITHOUT HIM – PART 1"

Ameesha had just walked through the door of Cantrell's house. She had given up her place and started living at his because it was easier to manage his accounts and things from the computer in his home. Furthermore, Cantrell literally had a house full of money. She knew that he said he didn't run the streets anymore but when he did, he must have run them hard. He told her to just spend his money as she saw fit until he could get out of this mess. He asked her to resign from the club, handle his affairs for him, and to take care of his seed that was in her stomach. She was now 4 1/2 months pregnant and things just weren't looking good for Cantrell. She was totally lost with no one to call on for help. Even Lil Lonzo missed Cantrell. He didn't understand why he couldn't come home with them when they would visit him, but Cantrell always had her buy him new toys and games to keep his mind off of him for the time being.

She had just left his lawyers office, only to find out that Cantrell was being charged with an almost 20-year-old murder. The state had already dismissed the gun charges, but he had been sitting for the last few months awaiting trial on the murder. His attorney, Mr. Goldstein, had also informed her that the state had a witness by the name of Trevor Bledsoe aka Bleed that wrote a statement saying that he saw Cantrell kill whoever this Arab person was. He also said that Cantrell used to brag about the killing as if he gained some sort of street credibility from it. Mr. Goldstein said that even though the gun charges were dismissed, Cantrell still had a criminal record, and with this being viewed as almost a racially motivated hate crime, it would be very hard to win this case with someone of his own race pointing the finger at him. Ameesha was distraught. She had nowhere to turn, and the only person that she knew from the streets was Sylvia. That was it, she would call Sylvia and ask her if she knew some person named Bleed.

CHAPTER THIRTY-TWO

"LIFE WITHOUT HIM – PART 2"

Sylvia had been trying to get an address on Ameesha for two weeks straight. Not going to school with someone and then trying to find them was proving to be very stressful. She didn't know a single person that knew Ameesha, except for Morgan, and Morgan didn't really know anything about her personal life. Ameesha was just an older friend who took a liking to Morgan back in their private school days. At this point, she was 100% convinced that Renzo's death, along with Cantrell and Bleed's disappearances were connected. She needed answers. Bleed was her everything, he was all that she knew. On her bad days, she could just have Bleed come over so that she could sit on his face and reliever her stress. Even on her good days she enjoyed sitting on his face. Outside of missing him and needing him sexually, his presence had always been what made life worth living for her. He saved her from being just another lost and abused girl and made her a woman, his woman.

She didn't want to get forceful with Ameesha, but it

was time for her to spill the fucking beans. Sylvia started to get emotional and that usually didn't happen to her. She could take a person's life rather it be a man, woman, or child, and not think twice about it, but right now she was headed towards an emotional meltdown. Ameesha better fucking come....... (Sylvia's phone rang).

"Hello, is this Sylvia?" Ameesha said on the other end.

"Yes, who is this?" Syl replied.

"It's Ameesha. I'm so sorry that I've been distant." Ameesha said while crying. "My life is in shambles. Cantrell has been in jail for months now on some trumped-up gun charges, but he beat that case. I thought that he would be released, but I just got word from his attorney that some man named Trevor Bledsoe is fingering him for a 20-year-old murder. I have no one to turn to, and I'm just lost. I'm five months pregnant, and I'm over here falling to pieces. If you know anyone who knows this Trevor person, can you have them to ask him why does he want to do this to my Cantrell and my babies, why?"

Sylvia was speechless… this explained so much. Bleed must be in some sort of witness protection program or something, and that's why he didn't contact her. Well, at least he was alive and when all of this is over, she would get to see and hold him again. She had mixed feelings though. She had grown to love Ameesha, and she hated to see her hurting like this, but shit without her man she was hurting too. She decided not to tell her that she knew Bleed that was out of the question."Calm down Meesh. I know a lot of the street people in the city; I will keep my eyes and ears open for you. I will get back with you really soon. Is this a good number to reach you on?" Syl asked.

"Yes." Ameesha said, still sobbing.

"Ok, you keep it together over there and let me see what I can do!" Syl responded.

Ameesha tried to pull herself together and said, "Thanks Sylvia… thank you so much."

"No problem Sis, no problem." Syl said.

Sylvia thought to herself, *"Fuck what she is talking about. I need to be with Bleed… why did he leave me? Why didn't he take me with him?"*

CHAPTER THIRTY-THREE

"SELFISH"

"Stay here at this cabin and don't call anyone from that phone." Detective Stanton barked at Bleed. "This is a high-profile case, and I'm pretty sure that Mr. Solomon has someone in his corner that would love to put a bullet in your head."

Bleed said, "Yeah yeah yeah. The same drill as the motel."

He watched the detective walk to his car and get in. Bleed thought about what the detective was saying and laughed to himself. He had been secretly using a cell phone that he convinced the little fat girl who worked at the motel's front desk to buy for him two months ago. He had unlimited calling, text, and the Internet. He laughed again because he knew that he was Cantrell's shooter, and he damn sure wasn't going to put a bullet in his own head. Cantrell had gotten old with no real connection to the streets, so he had no one to call upon. Even with all the money in the world, he wouldn't have a clue as to who he could pay to get him touched. He was nothing more than a pawn at this point and the added plus of him, sitting in the county jail didn't help him much either.

Bleed walked into his uncle's old cabin. It seemed like years since he had been there. The place had that scent that you would smell in an older person's home: the old furniture, cigarettes and cigar smell. Cob webs were all over the place. They gave him that eerie haunted house feeling as if he were about to find a skeleton in one of the empty bedrooms. To his surprise, there was a bottle of grey goose sitting on the kitchen counter. It had to be over 8 years old. He peeked down into the basement; the pool table was still there. He had figured that one of his aunts who had access to the place would have sold everything in it that was worth taking by now since his uncle passed, but that was not the case. It was here that he taught Sylvia, the love of his life, how to shoot a gun. She had a lot of built-up anger in her from childhood family issues, and that anger fueled her desire to learn to shoot. Bleed taught her well. He wanted her to always be able to protect herself, even in his absence. He also paid for her to take Krav Maga, in which she earned a black belt. It was amazing to him that she maintained her girly appearance and mannerisms after going through such harsh training. He laughed and thought about how Sylvia kicked ass. She had martial arts competition trophies that stood taller than her.

Ever since Detective Stanton had moved him out to West Virginia in a witness protection program six months ago, he hadn't talked to Sylvia or anyone else for that matter. Living up there alone in a rinky dink motel gave him a lot of time to think. He had close to a million dollars still stashed in his van. He figured that he and Sylvia could just leave Cincinnati, possibly even move up north to Michigan. He figured that he could go to school to be an electrician, and perhaps she could go to hair school, and they would open her up a salon. He would eventually purchase a work van and start his own electrical contracting company. He longed to be with Sylvia. It had been over six months since he had been with her, and he needed to be with her now so that he could take his mind off of the fact that he had to take the stand against a man who showed him nothing but love from day one. He tried to figure a way out of it all that would allow everyone to win, but sinking Cantrell was the only way that he could save himself as well as Sylvia.

It was almost a 2-hour drive from the hood out to the cabin. He wondered if Sylvia would drive up to see him if she knew that he was back in town. To call her though, would mean that he would have to discuss taking the stand against Trell, and he really didn't want to do that. Sylvia was from the hood. She understood the hood rules, and she would look down on him for taking the stand. No man should ever take the stand against another man; that's just how they were all raised in the hood. He wondered how she would feel if he explained that Detective Stanton was all prepared to lock her away forever as well had he not cooperated. He began to wonder would he had still flipped if Sylvia wasn't involved. He still had a chance to take back his statements and just take whatever he had coming, but then there was still Syl, where would that leave her? He decided that all he could do was call. Sylvia wasn't one to bite her tongue; if she truly felt a way about him, good or bad, she would express it upfront. He picked up his phone, scrolled down to her name, and after hesitating for over 2 minutes, he finally pushed the call button. After several long rings that seemed to last for hours, she answered the phone in a half sleep tone, "Bleed, is this really you?"

CHAPTER THIRTY-FOUR

"LOYALTY"

Sylvia took this ride too many times with Bleed and Fred. She had been taking this ride ever since she was a little girl. She thought back to the day when she passed her driver's exam, and Bleed let her drive him and Fred up to the cabin in Fred's Camaro. They kept rooting for her to speed once they made it to the dirt roads out near Clinton County. She remembered doing 100 miles per hour, and it still feeling as if she was doing 35. If her memory served her correctly, they had made the 2-hour drive that day in 1 hour and 15 minutes. Things were so simple and fun back then. Bleed wasn't her lover yet, he was her big brother and protector. That's why she truly believed him when he said that he had to give up Cantrell to save her. He would do anything to keep her alive and free, and she loved him for that. She figured that he must be embarrassed as well as stressed, because all of his street credibility and glory went down the drain in one seemingly bad chess move. His life would be over as he knew it after court at 10am tomorrow. She wondered if he had an escape plan. He couldn't think that he could publicly sink Cantrell and just come back to the hood as if everything is cool? The one thing that Sylvia knew about the streets was that reputation was everything. A whole lot of males and females hid behind reputations. She knew that the guy who was the quickest to shoot, or even the guy with the most bodies could bleed just like their victims. The one thing that saved them was that reputation and rumors made people scared to try them. To most, it seemed like their bullets wouldn't work against the harder guys, or a girl's punches wouldn't hurt the tougher girls, simply because of embedded fear based on reputation. Cooperating with the police would strip Bleed of his reputation. He would be viewed as a bitch, and all of his old enemies would line up to take shots at him. As strong and fearless as Bleed was his entire life; not only for himself, but for her too, she knew that this was the one time that he was scared to death.

Sylvia knew what she must do for him… she must give him the best pussy that her body could muster. He needed to release, and she would allow him to abuse her like a rag doll, fuck her like a $40 bop, and then release his load deep into her love vault for safe keeping. The thought of Bleed inside of her made her body quiver. She hadn't been touched by him in months. He was the only lover that she had ever known and her body yearned for him. She felt a tingling feeling in her toes that told her that they wanted to be in his mouth; the warmth of her pussy told her that it wanted his tongue to cool it off. Her mouth watered for a taste of his long black pole, and her tongue cried out wanting to massage the veins in his shaft. She almost squirted in her tights thinking about him. She was so caught up in the moment that she didn't even notice the black Mercedes tailing her with just its daytime running lights on. She pulled up to the familiar cabin. Normally, this was a place for all of them to come to relieve stress in other ways, like shooting and hunting. Tonight would be different. Sylvia was his woman, for better or worse, and she was all the stress relief that he needed. As she got out of the car, she wondered how Bleed would look. Would the stress have aged him a little over these rough six months? Would having the weight of the world upon his shoulders make him look beat down? Her questions were answered instantly when he opened the door for her.

"Baby!" she yelled, hopping up into Bleed's arms while throwing her legs around his waist.

He held her close and said, "Baby I missed you so much. You are the very reason that I..."

Sylvia stopped him mid-sentence and said, "Babe I'm sure that you made what you felt was the best decision for you, and us. As your woman, I stand behind any decision that you have made until the end. I'd die for you Bleed, so you already know that I will ride for you. Step back and let me luck at you, I haven't seen you in forever."

He laughed and said, "I buffed up a bit. All that I could do while I was living in that hell hole of a motel was use their weight room and do push-ups before bed." Bleed took off his T-shirt and Sylvia's mouth dropped. He was huge, at least 20lbs of solid muscle bigger than he was the last time that she had seen him. His abs were chiseled like the statues of the Greek gods. She was eager to be body to body with him, so she ripped off her shirt and reached in for a hug. Bleed stared into her eyes, and he felt that he could see deep into her soul. She wasn't judging him; she was simply there to love and support him. Bleed held both sides of her face and gently kissed her lips. She opened her mouth for his second kiss, and he stuck his tongue deep into her throat. He felt her body relax as if she was ready to give her all to him, and he obliged. He picked Syl up and sat her on the island counter in the kitchen, kissing her intensely as he carried her. She, too, put on weight, in a good way. Everything on her body was thicker: her thighs, ass, and her breast had all grown significantly. He pushed her in the middle of her chest signaling for her to lean back. He took a long slow lick starting from her navel, up to her stomach, and over her breast, stopping at her neck. He nibbled hard on her neck, biting in a manner that was right at the pain threshold of hurting her really well. Syl couldn't believe it; she had never felt such intensity from Bleed before. The way that he held her was driving her wild. She couldn't move a muscle; he was standing in between her legs holding her arms tight with brute force as he nibbled on her neck. Sylvia felt her pussy drip. She had just came before even being penetrated. Her clitoris was on fire. She wanted his tongue to douche it so bad, but her neck was on fire as well, and he was tending to that fire. Bleed let go of her arms and got down on his knees motioning for her to stand over him. She stood over him and his mouth was the perfect resting place for her hot pussy. She wanted her every drop to cover his face. She wanted him to drain all the juices that she had stored inside of her for the six long months since she had seen him. His tongue was plunging into her wetness, and every so often he would pleasure her clitoris with the tip of it. She felt her leg shake; she was having another orgasm. This time it was all going to drip into his mouth and down his face. Sylvia bit her lip hard, focusing on her orgasm; she wanted the pressure to go away, but the intensity was euphoric. She needed the release! At that very moment, something inside of her exploded and all six months of her love nectar came gushing out. She didn't even have to hold his head to make sure that he got it all because he was holding the back of her thighs, making sure that he lapped up every sweet drop. He stood up and noticed that she had painted his face, he looked like a beautiful piece of artwork. Every muscle on his body was hardened, and all ten inches of his man hood stood directly out in front of him. The tip was swollen and red as if it was trying to force him to stretch 3 more inches. She could see the veins in it, and they looked like lightning bolts. He was going to hurt her for sure, and she welcomed it. She wanted to relieve his pain and relieve his stress. She wanted him to punish her for everything that the world was doing to him, and as if he was reading her mind, he granted her wish.

Bleed grabbed her by the waist, lifting her off of her feet. While still standing, he slowly lowered Sylvia down onto his fully erect penis. He only allowed her three easy thrust before he tore into her. He was throwing his dick into her, bouncing her up and down on his manhood as if he was bouncing a basketball with two hands. She thought that her insides were going to rip, and she loved it! She felt like a rag doll as he slung her all around the cabin. She tried to kiss him, but he was too focused on digging deep into her. This was the dick that she craved for months, that I'm mad at the world dick.

She tried to whisper to him, "Take it all out on me baby!" however, with each thrust, he took her breath away so her words never materialized. He was slinging his manhood like Tre did his arms in the movie Boys in the Hood, but instead of jabbing the air, he was jabbing her sweet spot, hitting the back on every thrust. If someone was to ask her how many times had she came, her reply would have been that she was in one long continuous state of orgasm. She came on his tip every time he struck gold at the back of her vagina. Syl thought that she heard a noise outside of the cabin, but she was having to hard of a time trying concentrating on taking the dick and listening for the noise.

Bleed's legs gave out on him, so he put Syl down. He backed up, sat down in a chair, and closed his eyes to take it all in. He wondered what the noise was outside of the cabin as well, but he assumed it was an animal. Sylvia walked towards him in a seductive manner, grabbed his fully erect penis, and sat down on it slowly. She listened to the crackling sound of her wetness, and squeezed him with her pussy to make sure that she stimulated every nerve in his penis. She started thrusting her hips, taking Bleed to another world full of pleasure. She felt him in her stomach, and after two more thrust she could have sworn that she felt him in her heart. Bleed tried to talk, but he could barely get out the words, "I'm cuuummmmminnng!" There was a loud boom, the 45 caliber hand gun sounded like dynamite had gone off in the room. Blood was splattered all over the wall, and brains were scattered throughout the kitchen area by the island. The aura of death filled the room, and an eerie silence covered the entire cabin like a blanket.

Sylvia stared down at Bleeds lifeless body in total disgust; she wanted to spit on him. She stood over Bleed still holding the 45 that she had strategically placed on the window sill by the chair, knowing that she would eventually ride him there. His brains were blown completely into the next room. Half of his face was gone, and he was still cumming. She made sure she hopped up before even a single drop of his rat semen entered her. Her eyes were filled with tears, and her heart was loaded with mixed emotions. Bleed had been so caught up in the pleasure of his orgasm that he never noticed that Syl had slid the gun off of the sill while riding him. She loved Bleed with all of her heart, but he lost his manhood and his fucking mind. No real man would take another man away from his family and kids, and hand him over to the cops as if his life had no value. Nah, to be associated with a nigga like that went against everything that Syl had ever learned in the streets. She kept thinking about Ameesha crying on her shoulder wondering how she was going to manage having a child who would never get to see its father free because of Bleed. His weak ass may not have kept his brother, but she was damn sure her sister's keeper.

Sylvia knew for sure now that she heard a noise outside. She crept to the window and peeked out without moving the curtain but saw nothing. She wondered how she could explain her DNA all over the damn place when they found Bleed's body. She wondered if she could turn the gas on and somehow start a fire on the porch that would blow up the entire cabin. She walked over to the stove and turned the burner knob, and just like she thought, the gas was off. She heard the sound from outside again, then she heard footsteps on the porch. She wasn't about to do life if the police were on the other side of that door. If it was a Good Samaritan who had just so happen to hear the gunshot, he or she would die too. She heard someone call her name...

"Syllll Sylll, open the door! I am here to help you, and I'm unarmed." The unknown person said.

Sylvia peeked out of the curtain and saw a face that she had seen before... someone that she knew was in Cantrell's corner whom she could trust, and she opened the door. In walked the African from the gas station, Maarku, and he was holding two gas cans.

"Put on something, grab your things, and back your car out a little bit away from the house. I heard the shot, looked through the window and saw you standing over him. Move quickly, we have to clean this up fast!" Maarku explained.

Sylvia did as he instructed. Once she was outside, she saw Maarku pouring gas all over Bleed's body and throughout the entire cabin. He came outside with one gas can, and ran towards a tree on the side of the house. He climbed the tree like a long-armed monkey and got up on the roof. He poured gas all over the roof and set the fire. He scurried back down the tree and set fire to the house as well. He jogged over to where she was leaning against the car, stood in front of her, and said, "You have done a noble deed. Few women can put what must be done before their hearts and emotions. I have been following you for two weeks. I followed you here because I knew that the rat would contact you at some point before the trial. When I saw you hit the highway going dead east, I knew you were headed to him. What I didn't know was that you were going to exterminate the rodent yourself. I planned to murder him when you both had drifted off to sleep, but now I bow to you my queen. Cantrell is my brother; we are bound by a pact that is deeper than blood, and you went to bat for him. I offer you my heart, soul, and my riches. That car right there is a 2014 550 Mercedes Benz. I don't even want you to drive your Impala back home, it is no longer fit for a woman of your caliber. I would be honored to have you accept the Mercedes as a gift and to have you drive it home tonight. You are a rare woman and these American men will never do right by you. Even though I have a wife at home, the customs and traditions of my country allow me to have more than one wife. Tonight, I get down on my knees in the most humble way and ask you would you be my wife?"

REMEMBER...

When the smoke cleared, everyone looked for the queen but she was nowhere to be found. Some looked thinking that she would be behind the king, but she was not there. Some looked around the king to see if she was by his side, but she wasn't there either. Everyone looked out in front of the king thinking that she was somewhere in front of him, but there was still no sign of the queen. There were those in the crowd who never took their eyes off of the king, those were the seers. They never had to look for the queen because they saw her right in front of them. The queen had emerged with her divine counterpart, and now they could see her reflection in the greatness of the king.

Made in the USA
Lexington, KY
18 March 2019